TO
CAROL,
with much appreciation
for her support.
with gratitude &
blessings,
Katharine

250 920 5708

KNGENIE @
shaw, ca

TESTIMONIALS

"This fascinating book is a kaleidoscope of perspectives on life from childhood and war, to immigration to Canada, to having a son gifted with schizophrenia and flights of imagination, and of coming to terms with herself, her multifaceted and intermittently extremely painful life. Katharina's book is a most rewarding read."

Dr. Roland H. Guenther, PhD MD(Germany), Homeopath

———————————————❦———————————————

"Katharina Nolla has a wonderful, rich way of expressing herself. We follow Leni's journey of growth through the many experiences life offers, both good and bad. Finally, Leni reaches serenity, surrounded by the peace and beauty of British Columbia."

Anneli Driessen PHD, PHD, MCC
President and CEO of the International Metaphysical
Academy, Inc. and Sacks International, Inc.
www.maxsacks.com www.annelidriessen.com
www.metaphysicalacademy.com

———————————————❦———————————————

"I love this book! I walked with Leni all the way through, experiencing her happiness, the horrors of war and dealing with the puzzlement of why it all happened. Through no fault of her own her life was cruelly turned upside down. She spends many years trying to come to terms with the random nature of life and finds a rich spiritual well of wisdom."

Sally Jennings, Professional Editors Assn of Vancouver Island

———————————————❦———————————————

"Katharina, I'm amazed by all you have gone through and how you've come out the other end! This book portrays a truly valiant spirit as she pursues her own challenging journey to inner peace."

Ann Moffat

ACKNOWLEDGMENT

BOOK cover design taken from the painting entitled "Deep Peace Journey" by Lalita C. Lane.

Edited by Sally Jennings, Professional Editors Assn of Vancouver Island. In her absence, by Robin Alys Roberts Professional Editors Assn of Vancouver Island. With further assistance by my friends Paulina Karsh, Andrea Clark, Susan Scott, Pat Miller, Ann Moffat, Mavelous Trudeau and her lovely daughter Michelle. Wolfgang Zilke, and Jim Roth who spent unaccountable hours in bailing me out from my computer challenges, and his beautiful wife Jian Ping who patiently stood by.

To my two precious children whom I had the privilege to give birth. My children are my greatest teachers.

Messages from the Periphery

A WORK OF LITERARY FICTION BASED ON

MY PERSONAL EXPERIENCES

IN SEARCH OF MYSELF

Katharina Nolla

Please find more information at
www.insearchofmyselfsite.wordpress.com

ISBN: 978-0-9959146-0-5

Cover design by Iryna Spica
Typeset in *Sabon* with *Work Sans* and *Script* display at SpicaBookDesign.

Printed in Canada by Printorium Bookworks/Island Blue,
Victoria B.C.

TABLE OF CONTENTS

Part Three. Messages from the Periphery

Part Four

AUTHOR'S NOTE

*"The philosophy of the wisest man that
ever existed is mainly derived from the
act of introspection."*

WILLIAM GODWIN

MESSAGES From The Periphery is a book of self-exploration in search of myself and contains the key to unlock my tucked-away emotions. It dates from the 1990s Balkan War up to the present, with intermittent childhood flashbacks to World War II, which devoured a great part of my childhood innocence.

Its pages reveal my deepest secrets, unveiled through my personal hardships and tribulations. It exposes the atrocities of ethnic cleansing, fueled by acts of terrorism which I had experienced. In the words of Robin Alys Roberts words Professional Editor of Vancouver Island, it takes us on a journey both through and beyond the physical and geographical, into the sweetness of forgiveness and positive forward movement.

A further venture explores the mysteries of the parallel worlds including her son's world of schizophrenia, which he perceives as a foreign invasion.

My intent is to encourage readers to journal their own pages of self-discovery to find their flow of wisdom as I sought to find myself. The words may be faint at first

– but one must have faith – as they will become clear and inspire confidence as you complete your own book of life. My advice is to listen to its messages. They are your greatest treasure, the vehicle of your transcendence.

If we aspire to become an advocate for peace, our primary responsibility is to check what other personalities we might have adopted along the way. Lurking inside, before they unleash their ammunition and explode in the future.

In the words of this book, you will discover your desires that drive you. Which desires that serve you, and which don't. Or that you have locked away? This is the mystery that is now beckoning on the dawning horizon, as the walls of the old paradigms are crumbling, and you reclaim your knowing.

Katharina Nolla

PART I

Moments in Time

MY NAME IS LENI

TIME is rapidly speeding up and greedily devouring my days and there is so much yet to be done. And I haven't bothered to check the expiry date of my earthly passport lately nor inquired about an option for renewal.

3:00 a.m. My mind spins like a Tibetan medicine wheel dredging up memories from the deep that wash over me with regret for things done and not done. My name is Leni Almador. At times, I have imagined running away from myself but there seemed nowhere else to go and as I listen in to others' stories, I question whether their position is any better or worse than mine.

MY INITIATION TO
THIS LIFE

MY Oma (grandmother) said when I emerged from my mother's womb, my pulse didn't beat as it should, in an early photo my eyes stare out in a state of shock.

The priest was called to pour the baptismal water over my head. The holy water was intended to save me from purgatory should my heart, prematurely expire. All the while politically instigated fireworks exploded in the nearby square, shaking the foundation of our house.

Warfare remained the background soundtrack throughout my childhood years. When I asked my Oma why people chose to wage war to fight and kill each other, she said, "Hopefully, your generation will have the wisdom to sort this out. Peace can neither be bought nor sold. Nor can it be purchased in the market place. It has to be a personal contribution."

Otati (grandfather) once told me, "People don't need to wage wars for survival. Most survive quite well; it's just who they are. He stared at the pipe he pulled from his pocket and said, "Once the fire is out, it's time to start another." Then he lit it.

Indoors, our domestic situation churned in a similar state of unrest. Family members constantly disagreed with one another. Our neighbour, Herr Boehm, declared that waging war was mankind's natural instinct, and others agreed.

It was a world that demanded unconditional allegiance to the Czar and unquestionable devotion to the church. Schools expected obedience and there was no interrupting the teacher with questions. The concern of "Who am I?" established itself early in my mind. When I asked my Tati (father) this question he laughed and replied, "Little Duchess, what kind of question is this? You are Leni, of course." He added that little girls shouldn't concern themselves with such questions but concentrate on being good.

I tried hard to be good and most of all I prayed for this war that was mutilating and killing many people, to end. I wondered why my prayers went unanswered. Maybe there were too many conflicting prayers from all warring sides that overloaded the communication lines to heaven.

From then on, I preferred to hold my own counsel and told no one my innermost thoughts. Instead, I withdrew into my secret place in the orchard where the honeysuckle and the blossoms of the fruit trees released their sweetness and the bees collected their pollen. Beings from another world visited me there. Who became my silent playmates and showed me glimpses of the other side. They produced tubes filled with light for me to play with I bent into various shapes, and could confide my thoughts without being laughed at. The orchard was also my escape when Tati and Otati had fierce arguments. The day Otati chased Oma, wielding an axe, I hid in a tree as she was whisked away to hide with relatives.

One day, I overheard our housemaid, Ivanka, mumble to Ljuba, who came to help with the laundry. "A shame, she was never the same after the accident." Ivanka was referring to my mother whom people described as fragile as a Dresden doll. Sometimes she confined herself to her room propped in bed, her skin pale. The shades were drawn – in a house of silence.

I asked Oma, "What did Ljuba mean about the accident?" Because Ljuba alluded to my having a sibling, I also asked, "Did I have a little brother once?

"Never ask this question in front of Mother," she replied. "You wouldn't want to upset your mother, would you?"

No, I don't want to upset anyone, especially my mother.

MY GEOGRAPHICAL
HISTORY

WE lived in Slavonia – a province of Croatia, adjacent to the grassy plains of the Hungarian puszta (steppes) where Genghis Kan's hordes once thundered. On a clear day, when we reached the border, we could see the landmark levers on the other side that had long ropes with buckets attached, ready to be lowered into the wells to draw water. They would be emptied into wooden troughs for the grazing sheep and cattle to drink. Further on, in the swampy parts, flocks of marsh birds took to the sky, serving as a hunting ground during the season.

The puszta with its seemingly never-ending space seemed such a romantic place. Here various occupations have left their mark. The wind has free range and trained dogs hold the grazing sheep in line.

Here the legendary czikos – Hungarian cowboys – galloped at great speed to keep their long-horned cattle in check, that hundreds of years ago had made the crossing over the Carpathian Mountains.

Our province has a continental climate of freezing cold winters and hot summers. With acres of wheat stretching to the horizon, this region was considered the bread-basket of Europe. Wild boars roamed the forest.

In the seventeenth century, after the Turks had been defeated and driven from the region, the desire for agricultural cultivation arose. At that time, my ancestors emigrated here from Germany. We became Yugoslav citizens and swore allegiance to the Czar, but were entitled to speak our language and retain our culture from the homeland. We identified ourselves as Donauschwaben (Germans from the Danube). Njemacki or Svapski, to the Slavs. Immigrant life was difficult and perilous, but eventually through hard work and perseverance, we prospered.

My favourite times were the summers spent at our estate called Berak. Although it was originally built for a bishop, Tati had purchased it from a Hungarian landowner.

Tati would take me along when he visited the shepherd who lived in a small mobile house in the acacia grove and who would play the flute with Tati singing along, his perfect white teeth flashing. There I met the children from the nearby hamlet, where I befriended Anica and Helena – both my age. Their houses had dirt floors and on Saturday afternoons, their mothers would cheerfully stir a mixture of cow dung and lime in a bucket, which they spread over the firmly-pounded dirt floors to keep the insects away.

They baked their bread in outdoor clay ovens. The ingredients were a mixture of coarse flour with a variety of whole grains mixed in. After my first bite, I asked Tati, "Can we bake this bread at our home?"

"What an odd request," my guests answered. Wondering why I would prefer this coarse brown bread to our privileged, refined white bread with its crispy crust?"

From then on, I would bring one of our freshly baked loaves in exchange for a chunk of Anica's. Anica's mother said, "She is one of us!" They all laughed good-naturedly.

At times, however, Helena looked on with a sullen expression or turned and walked away. But the rest of us were having too much fun to pay attention to her behaviour; we simply enjoyed our visit and our ritual by munching on our exchanged delicacies.

It was on these visits that I would bring along my doll for Helena and Anica to play with. I called my doll Tatiana, because I liked the sound of Russian names. At times I would confide my secrets to her. She had real human hair and large blue eyes that opened and closed. This fascinated my playmates, since their dolls were made from worn-out socks stuffed and tied in two places so that one produced the head, the other the torso, with arms and legs sewn on. One day, I saw Helena secretly pull some strands of hair off Tatiana's head, which made me sad.

Sometimes, Tati and I rode on his favourite horse, the wind whispering in our hair. Or we raced through the plains in a beautiful carriage that came from Hungary, with Anica beside me as my guest.. Tati's friend Herr Baumann, who owned three stores, thought that Berak should make enough money for father to buy a shiny car like his, but we enjoyed riding in the carriage.

The winters are a recollection of sleigh rides gliding through a landscape with the shrubs and twigs magically coated with ice, glistening like cathedral chandeliers. We huddled under brick-heated fur blankets, while the horses pranced with rhythmic grace, their breath exhaling ghostly wreaths to float through the air. This was also the time when Tati would go out to hunt partridges in the marshes. On the mantelpiece hung the head of a wild boar that he had shot, its face frozen in a perpetual grin.

That's how life was before history took a sharp turn and Tati was enlisted as a soldier because the Germans were bombing the streets of Belgrade. We saw him off to the station wearing the imperial Chetnik uniform to fight the invading Germans alongside the Serbs, Croats and the inhabitants from the mountain regions. Everyone looked sad and worried. Mother cried and Tati said he would be back.

At the beginning, the odd letter would arrive from the front, but soon all communication ceased. What if we didn't see him again?

"He will be back," I kept telling myself. "He will be back."

One day there was shouting and I heard the urgency of running feet outside. Someone called, "They're coming!" In the distance a group of soldiers became visible. As they came closer, I could make out the beards that obscured their faces. Some raised their rifles, firing shots into the air. The women came running. "Look out, they've been drinking," they said. One of the bearded men called out, "My little duchess!" There was only one person who called me that.

"Tati," I cried out while we ran towards each other, with mother running right behind me. His strong arms swung me in the air while I snuggled against his chest and his other arm reached out to encircle mother's waist, and we all laughed and so did the sun shining down. Daffodils nodded their heads. Tulips displayed their multitude of colours. The church bells began to ring in celebration and I came to understand that Tati and his fellow soldiers had become German prisoners of war but had now been released. The Czar had fled the country and a new leader named Ante Pavic had taken his place in Croatia, whose armed forces were called Ustashe, who had formed an

KATHARINA NOLLA

alliance with Germany. From there on, the Croats were enlisted into the ranks of the Ustashe, the ethnic Germans like my Tati, the Wehrmacht, with no choice in-between.

But the Chetniks who remained loyal to the Czar weren't happy with the change. They regrouped in the mountains, and soon another name crossed everyone's lips. Josip Broz, short for Tito, who had his own ideas, with a following called Partisans.

Never mind the political situation, it was Easter and I had my Tati back to protect me. And this was supposed to be the war that for the second time was to end all wars on this planet of God's creation.

Herr Baumann visited in his shiny car and we drove out into the countryside, continuing on to Berak. Mother untied her hair, allowing the breeze to ruffle its lovely flow, while her silk scarf, tied to the car's antenna, fluttered like a dove. Our laughter rang as clear as the church bells that were tolling. I always associate my Tati's homecoming with the renewal of spring and the day of Jesus' resurrection. At some point, all sides appeared to settle down. The German occupation and the Chetniks seemed aligned, the Chetniks and the Partisans who likewise vied for power, experienced a moment's friendship. The Wehrmacht, Uatashe and the Italians managed to arrive at some sort of understanding. Then everyone changed their mind - and then again, blaming each other for the breakdowns and the atrocities committed. Soon it became unsafe to drive through the countryside. Trains were derailed or hijacked or bombed to burst into fireworks. At night, we heard deep rumblings and the rattling of machine guns from the countryside. The Chetniks and the Partisans retaliated by blowing up bridges and trains, and setting houses and factories on fire. It was as though a grey sheet had obscured the once clear sky. I was shown a mound in the backyard camouflaged with shrubs and other vegetation, called a bunker, with a secret entry.

At bed time, I had to lay out my clothes in a certain order: cardigan, dress, petticoat, stockings, with the undergarments arranged on top of the pile, easy to slip into. This routine was in preparation to run for the bunker, with instructions not to wait for anyone, in case of another nightly Chetnik raid. Or by what this time could have been initiated by the Partisans. Where loved ones were dragged never to return, or having their throat slit. The Partisans were initially difficult to identify, wearing looted clothes in place of uniforms. It was the first time we had seen girls and women in the ranks of combat. One of them who walked away was wearing mother's fur-lined coat.

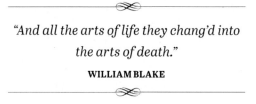

"And all the arts of life they chang'd into
the arts of death."
WILLIAM BLAKE

Fast-forward to November 1992 – Second Balkan War.
Journaled from my home in Victoria.

For years, I have acted as a pillar of strength, while tucking away my distressful childhood memories in the protective web I have spun around myself. But this day watching the current news broadcast from Sarajevo (Bosnia Herzegovina's capital in my former homeland) suffering under a siege of rubble and despair. The prosperous port town of Vukovar, known for its beautiful baroque architecture, has become a stretch of wasteland, ravaged by the impact of the current 1990's Second Balkan War. This news is testing my complacency and stirring up memories about how an unresolved past will indeed retrieve its ammunition to repeatedly explode in the future – spitting back its pent-up hatred and greed for dominance.

These conflicts are triggering childhood memories: I saw my Oma grabbed by the hair – her head jerked back so that only the whites of her eyes were visible. "When did you last see him?" they demanded. "Where is he hiding?"

It was the Partisan's doing the interrogating this time. They demanded to know about her nephew, Drago, whom they accused of supplying their adversary the Croat Ustashe with flour from his mills. Each time Oma had no answer, the assault was repeated until I feared her neck would snap. By then the tactics of warfare were no mystery. An initiation absorbed by osmosis made it clear even to a child, that had Drago supplied the other side it would have determined his fate in a like manner. From then on in, some family members became politically divided and took up arms against each other.

This was the case in my own family. Another interrogator kicked mother with such force that she stumbled and hit the floor, blood oozing from her mouth. I stood by, feeling a bitter lump in my throat and instinctively realized that one day I might spit it out with no guarantee where it would land. Right then – nine years of age – I made a vow: That the impact of warfare must be exposed, its stories revealed, and all sides be sure to listen and to be heard.

It begs an answer to a previous question, "doesn't the world care?" which I once asked. It is no longer a matter of whether the world cares, but whether we are willing to change?

And who says we are too small to make a difference?

Yet there was once a time of sweet laughter, of tables laden with food, homes where families planned their children's future and swapped fruit and vegetables over the fences.

This memory dates back to the time when it was intermittently safe to travel. When mother and I visited relatives in the beautiful port town of Vukovar during the summer of 1944. Being a child of the plains with few rivers marking the landscape, the sight of that mighty stream of the Danube, evoked astonishment as our train chugged over a gigantic bridge spanned with graceful arches.

Heavily laden barges drifted lazily into the distance while in the harbour, skiffs with puffed-up sails bobbed on the waves, as colourful as the butterflies clustering on flowers along the boulevard. Peals of laughter rang from the occupants of stately yachts. Along the bank, one could dine on fresh-caught fish cooked crispy brown, tender and juicy inside, and for dessert my favourite, *gibanica*, curd cheesecake. It was a time when the various ethnicities still celebrated their differences and contentment made good neighbours. But weeks later after our visit, news of an ethnic cleansing campaign against our relatives circulated from that region. Their property was confiscated and handed over as a reward to the encroaching Tito's Partisan warriors, by now clad in professional uniforms. News of Tito's death camps invoked sheer terror. When rumours about other camps in various regions around the globe began to sneak through. The collective propaganda machines were working overtime – some stronger than others – until no one was sure what was going on. Soon afterwards, all communications with my relatives ceased. We never heard from them again.

I overheard Tati in conversation with our neighbour, Herr Boehm, about this global madness. "There are two people telling the truth," said Herr Boehm. "The Fuehrer and his sidekick Propaganda Minister Joseph Goebbels." He lowered his voice – but I heard him say, "Lies!" So, was it all lies? What were they talking about?

What did he mean? "Who is telling the lies?" I asked.

"Jedermann, mein Kind," ("Everyone, my child,") he said.

Tati looked at him sternly, then turned to me and said, "Find something else to do, Leni."

It was later after the war that I came across the written words that I recognized as the quote Herr Boehm had mentioned, attributed to Goebbels. It said, "Make the lie big, make it simple, keep saying it, and eventually they will believe it." Ironically Hitler was to have said, "If you win, you need not have to explain...If you lose, you should not be there to explain!"

Now many years later as an adult, I recall Oma's answer to my question of why people chose to wage war to fight and kill each other. Her words ring back: "Hopefully your generation will have the wisdom to sort this out."

And here I am.

I am that generation and what can I say other than there is still much work to be done before we pass on. We who have experienced its impact should be the advocates to plant the seeds of change.

My dream is to inspire the young generation to say "No More!" to war. I hope they focus on preventive, not destructive revolution – no matter what race or nationality. May this be our intention – as we fill our cathedrals, temples, mosques and synagogues, as well as our inner sacred space. In response to my question, "Who says we are too small to make a difference?" – we can add, "YES, WE CAN!"

Say these words often. Say them out loud. Make them simple. Eventually they will come true. YES, WE CAN!

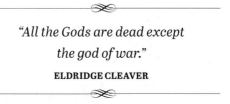

*"All the Gods are dead except
the god of war."*

ELDRIDGE CLEAVER

Contrary to what was preached at Sunday mass from the pulpit about loving thy neighbour as thyself and doing unto them as you would have done to you, I failed to process what my eyes had witnessed. I saw priests and cardinals bless the weapons to slay our neighbours. "Can't you see what you do to the others, you inflict on yourself," my child mind cried out, and searched for a solution that would end these armed conflicts. I imagined two soldiers from opposing sides, famished and weary with exhaustion, intermittently arriving on my doorstep and I would present two meals both portions served on one plate. I envisioned this becoming a regular frontline practice – two sides, two spoons and one plate so they could honestly each get to know one another for who they truly were without having to pretend or being judged otherwise, and have a chance to tell their stories.

However, this was not how it turned out. Too many self-appointed idealists stood in the way, hindering my vision of progress. The only difference was the alternating flags that served to "legitimize" the next regime change. Perhaps history should be written from the point of view of a child not yet proficient in political rhetoric. Now, many years later, I ask whether examining the past is a waste of time.

This depends on my purpose and on questioning my intent. Is it my intent to tenaciously cling to my interpretations to keep alive, or is it about dismantling my personal ammunition to dismantle at the border crossing into the future?

My intention is not to stir up additional dissension or take sides against one over the other, but encourage each other to consider whether this is the kind of legacy we want for our children: a world with no place they can either call home or trust? Parents who are unable to shield them from memories their minds will not be able to erase.

As long as even one child is traumatized, the whole human race is traumatized and suffers. As a survivor – with a history similar to millions of others, this is my story. The difference is in the processing. It is my responsibility to monitor my own reactions and examine what I might feed into my system. What residual layers might I have accumulated? I may find it isn't always as rosy inside as I project to the world. Therefore, I must not overlook and waste the wisdom of my experiences, but ask what they have taught me. This attempt could apply to all aspects of my life.

THE SPACES
IN-BETWEEN

April 1992, Journaled from my home in Victoria, B.C.

BREAKFAST is my time for introspection, exclusively reserved for me in my sunroom. There's a majestic old cedar tree in my backyard, ensuring my privacy. At the moment, the silence is interrupted by the sound of a lawnmower bursting into activity, intruding on my ritual. The seagull couple nesting on the roof sends a barrage of insults at the nearby crows eyeing their young fledglings as lunch.

My neighbour Angie peers through the sunroom window. I let her in. She is looking for her cat, Pesto. We check the basement, then the garden shed that a racoon family has claimed as their home. Angie's eyes settle on my son Jonathan, leaning against the shed.

"With that streamlined body and thick hair spilling over his forehead, he could have been a model," she says, with what seems like a tone of regret. She knows that sometimes he will disappear and then suddenly reappear, at times looking in need of repair.

"Sometimes I wonder how you cope, especially when he seems to withdraw into his world where he can't be reached," she says.

What could I say? I am the mother and it is a mother's job to persevere where others fail.

Schizophrenia: The impact of the diagnosis crashed down like a thunderbolt, splitting the foundation of my mind stamped with the medical approval. Initially I had dismissed his behaviour as a regular teenage transition. After all, Jonathan's familial genes aren't an exemplary proof of social conformity. This doesn't seem to run in our family and what defence mechanisms were available to me? I was raised in an environment where women were expected to endure their lot and, according to the priest, for those who prevailed without complaining, a reward would be waiting in heaven.

But trust was hard to come by, for some. Their tears dried up and expectations of compassion lay deeply buried. No one discussed the choice of inner healing or the treasures that can be found amongst the wreckage. The question of "am I to blame for my son's condition" is not an uncommon inquiry.

This time, I am challenged with a counter-question: "When you embark on a journey, do you always know where it will lead?"

If I have a map, my answer is, yes.

If I have a map, will I discover the unknown?

I have just returned from a visit to the hospital where Jonathan was committed for attempting to jump onto a moving train.

"Where do you think the train was headed?" I asked.

"Everybody is always full of questions," he said, "but rarely do they have the answer to their own," and on that note, his communication usually ends.

There is a trunk in my basement.
The trunk has a lock,
The lock has a key,
The key belongs to Jonathan.
He says it is the guardian of his memories.
Is this where we can meet?

Three days later, after I picked him up from the hospital and as I walked downstairs to throw the laundry into the dryer, Jonathan followed me. He unlocked the nearby trunk and removed some pages that he placed on a shelf. I was surprised because they were pages from his own personal journal.

"For you," he said, "you can read them, but only a few at a time."

After dinner, I asked him whether I could include some of his pages in the manuscript I was compiling for publication.

Intoduction of Page One from Jonathan's Journal (With His Permission)

After several days of dreary weather the sky is clearing. The sun flashes a stark whiteness like a Hiroshima explosion with no place to hide.

Who am I?

I am the son of a Catalan father raised in Barcelona, Spain, who was tall and blond and who according to mother kept some secrets stashed under his belt.

My mother, Leni, is German, and although she comes from a line of forebears with blue eyes and Aryan features, she has raven hair and slanted eyes and as I have observed, can keep no secrets.

Normalcy: The world demands a certain standard of normalcy, yet as I look around, no one seems clear how to deal with it and I feel I am living under a siege of a foreign invasion.

My therapist has this theory – if, by a certain age, a person doesn't feel securely integrated, they should expect pockets of disturbance to churn up in unexpected places.

According to my mother, when I was little, her marriage was failing and life was sending mixed messages. She believes these messages have been stitched into my emotional quilt. So she is working on her guilt. I try to separate myself from the system that shuts me out but it always seems to find a way of stuffing me back in.

Several days ago, I passed a church with a sign on the door that said, "Come in, those who are heavy laden" or something like that. I felt empty instead of laden but went in anyhow. My stomach had shrunk, so it looked like a mummy's. I hadn't eaten for over two days. There was a preacher in the pulpit preaching something about God helping those who helped themselves. My brain clicked off so I missed the rest of what was said but stuck around anyhow. With a gesture of the preacher's hand, as if it held a magic wand, a hush fell over the congregation, and sounds streamed from the pipe of the organ. It was a moment so soothing that I felt on the verge of fading away when a vision of juicy pizzas danced through my head. In the silence, two men rose from their seats, and walking

KATHARINA NOLLA

on padded soles, they each passed around a basket. When they reached my row, I dipped in to fund my dream of pizzas, helping myself just as the preacher had said. A commotion stirred through the seats and after a while two police arrived. That's how I ended up in the psych ward.

In the ward, there is this shadow of a man flitting through the hallways. Some of them come then leave, then come back again. "I can dissolve on command, you know," I heard him say. Being a shadow, nobody seems to pay attention to him except at pill time when they associate his medication with his name. Whenever he shows up, he sends me a sly smile.

This morning he paused and craning his scrawny neck, he scanned all corners. Satisfied we were alone, he beckoned, "Psst, psst." When I moved closer he whispered, "I know why you're here. There is a church connection to our story, you know."

"No, I don't know," I said.

"I am here because I dug up a flower from the park. Not for me, but for Him."

A smile danced across his face. "They found the plant, but they never found him, because I made sure I had him securely tucked away."

"Him?"

He flashed a conspiratorial smile. "The thing is I could tell he wanted to be with me – Jesus, that is." He vanished within himself then popped back briefly. After scanning the hallway again, he said, "When we get out of here, I'll introduce him to you." Then, as an afterthought he added, "By the way, my name is Saul – derived from the Bible – the man who fell off his horse and changed into Paul."

I mentioned this man, whose name is Saul turned Paul, to mother and her friend, Chuck.

"Sometimes he acts totally normal," I overheard Chuck remark one day, "then..." and here he paused to formulate his words, "at other times... gone."

No, it's better not to look into their mirror. The reflection becomes confusing. Once when I stepped into a store, the faces looked like wax-polished apples staring at me. I left the store and ran through the traffic with police sirens screaming through my head. I ran so fast that I landed at the military base, where they wanted me to walk a straight line. But I can't walk their line.

Saul-Paul says he can dissolve into the shadows, but who am I?

I am a possibility gone astray, with too many parts clanking and getting in each other's way.

I did run into Saul-Paul. It was several weeks after my discharge from the hospital. He wore an over-sized jacket, although the sun shone bright and hot. His eyes danced with excitement. "Come," he said, leading the way to a doorway in the alley.

He flung open his jacket and grinned. "See?" Against his heart, dangling from a leather string, hung a wooden carving of his Jesus, with red droplets painted on its brow. Tucked into the pocket of the lining was a small flowerpot, which evidently contained the dug-up plant from the park, containing one red flower, also sadly drooping. Mission accomplished, he turned and crossed the street amidst the rush-hour traffic, while cars honked their horns.

KATHARINA NOLLA

Saul-Paul has his Jesus. His purpose is to hide him and to nurture the potted flower. After all, life without purpose is an empty shell, prone to dubious squatters moving in.

There is a cosmic puzzle that haunts me. Christians say that Jesus is the Son of God. According to an alternate story, there was another son, Lucifer, of whom it was said he shone brighter than any star. Who for some obscure reason rebelled and, from there, was cast into darkness as deep as the Spanish Inquisition, woven into my father's history. Last night, on the table beside my bed, miniature cogs and wheels looking like the interior of a clock were neatly laid out. I know they were the pieces of my disconnected brain. When will the pieces be re-aligned again? Maybe on the day the two brothers reconcile in a lightening flash of bliss that will rock the sky, more powerful than any bomb, or any other manmade device.

Jonathan, Continued

December 1992

As soon as you are registered in the system, you are either categorized as stabi-lized, or de-stabi-lized – this is how my caseworker pronounces the words.

Lately, mother has been pre-occupied with the news about the current war in her birth country, the former Yugoslavia.

As the columns of refugees, trudge through a desolation littered with overturned and charred vehicles with a background of flames devouring their homes, mother is searching my eyes for an answer.

What can I say?

Stabi-lized, de-stabi-lized, each dragging their historical baggage along while President Clinton appears on the screen justifying his involvement, then flies home to play golf.

It's time to connect with my Maker, who some call God. "What do you have to say to all of this?" I ask.

But nothing clicks back.

I stare out of the window, even though there isn't much to see – just the neighbour's lawn like a carpet and someone clipping the shrubs. Then I hear a rustling inside my head. There is a shift in my brain, followed by a voice I recognize as His: "Those who slumber in a dream state cling to their interpretations transferred into the future. And this compulsion to take on the role of liberator by invading the territories of others is an illusion that places its own citizens under siege and taints their reputation. A peaceful country will not invade another."

After mother leaves the room, I switch the channel.

Willowy models saunter across the screen displaying the current fashion statements, switching life back to its present reality.

Leni

THE VICTORY

"O peace! How many wars were waged
in thy name?"
ALEXANDER POPE

Late 1943

IT was different at the beginning of the war, with a euphoric conviction that victory hung in the air. Soldiers had fastened flowers onto their helmets, trucks and motorcycles. Their uniforms looked smart and fresh. Cheering crowds appeared everywhere.

Months later, these uniforms looked worn and saggy. As I walked into my parents' room, a rucksack gaped on a chair between them and they were folding things into it. They smiled at me but it seemed limp and old. My Tati, who was "on leave," had to go back to be a soldier again. When I looked out the window, I saw our neighbour Frau Geber, standing in front of her house, her eyes red and swollen. She was watching her two handsome young sons who used to help wobbly Frau Weber totter across the street on a snowy day, and took me on sleigh rides. Now, bravely lined up in the square with rifles strapped to their shoulders, they stood ready to join the Russian front. It was the Fuehrer's ambition to conquer the world, and Russia was a big chunk of it.

WAR: War claims to defend life but clearly doesn't value life, while all sides insinuate then as now is fought for the sake of peace. If this were so, it seemed to me that judging by the numbers fought, there should be eternal peace by now. Simplistically, in war the participants reason that if their brothers or sisters, sons or daughters, fathers or mothers are participating, then surely it must be right for them too. As a result, millions of lives are still sacrificed on its altar, babies become orphans deprived of suckling at their mother's breasts. The music is drowned out by shell-fire, with no place to hide, and the playgrounds silenced. It transforms people you once knew, to become possessed by evil spirits. The only celebration is in the victory over another's defeat with a background of rubble where homes once stood. We tell our children that the other side is bad in order for us to look good. We justify our deeds so that we can lay down our heads, and go back to sleep.

I wondered what role could possibly be expected of Frau Geber's sons – because by then I understood that one side's victory meant brutal defeat and gruesome reprisals for the other.

On the other hand, the truth is crying for us to use the power of science and technology to create material equality for all.

THE CIRCUS

ONE day a troop of men rode into the square, performing acrobatic feats by standing upright on galloping horses. Others hung upside down or from the side attached to a strap, and I ran looking for my Tati. "Come, Tati, look, look," I called, tugging at his sleeve. "Men from the circus have arrived!" When he saw the horsemen, Tati laughed. "They are not from the circus," he said. "They are soldiers."

"What kind of soldiers are they, Tati?"

"They are Cossacks and have come from the Russian steppes to help fight the war to prevent communism from taking over."

When I looked closer, I could see the twin symbol ⚡⚡ (SS) lightning rod insignia on their caps. "Tati, why are wars fought?" I asked. "Are they wicked fairy tales in people's imagination?"

At that, he laughed. "With weapons, of course."

"Do they ever run out of weapons?"

"Mein Kind," he said (my child), do you ever run out of questions?" and he ruffled my hair and laughed again.

"We shall go on to the end, we shall fight in France,
We shall fight on the seas and oceans,
We shall fight with growing confidence and growing strength in the air, we shall defend

our Island, whatever the cost may be,
We shall fight on the beaches,
We shall fight on the landing grounds,
We shall fight in the fields and in the
streets,
We shall fight in the hills.
We shall never surrender, and even if,
which I do not for a moment believe,
this Island or a large part of it were
subjugated and starving, then our
Empire beyond the seas, armed and
guarded by the British Fleet, would carry
on the struggle, until, in God's good time,
the New World, with all its power and
might, steps forth to the rescue and the
liberation of the old."

WINSTON CHURCHILL

These are very passionate, strong words. Who wouldn't be inspired? But keep in mind that the other side feels just as strongly and passionately about their country. And there can be no war without the other willing to participate.

What if you don't make it back?

Linger in a rotten jail?

Come back with a limb missing, wishing you hadn't seen what you had to face, executed orders against the principles of your soul? In some cases, the only recognition paid is the moment their remains are returned.

KATHARINA NOLLA

What if their remains were never found to be properly buried, their spirit wandering through the valley of death in search of their other half?

If war is not a tangible matter, it is a powerful construct of the mind capable of shaping the world in the opposite direction.

Should I as an individual pick up a weapon and eradicate my other-minded neighbour, I would be accountable for my actions. Why then, do state-run institutions get away with it?

WHO IS IN CHARGE HERE?

"What is absurd and monstrous about war is that men who have no personal quarrel should be trained to murder one another in cold blood."

ALDOUS HUXLEY

Fast-backward to Spring 1944

OMA made it known that she did not approve of Drago and his wife Bianka's lifestyle. They entertained the "bohemian" crowd and spent too lavishly, she said – it was not how she was raised. What I remember about Bianca, were her graceful movements and the scent of her perfume evoking visions of balmy breezes, her carefree laughter trailing through the rooms on her visits. Once during her visit, I overheard Ivanka gossiping with Ljuba, saying that Bianca's mother liked to dance what sounded like the "Sharleston."

"What kind of dance is the Sharleston?" I asked Oma. She told me it was a dance that was too wild for a respectable woman to perform and showed too much leg. I would have liked to see Bianca's mother dance the Sharleston, but she never came for a visit.

Then one day, although we knew it wasn't safe to travel any longer, grandmother said that after all is said and done, Drago and Bianca were family and family bonds had to be respected where help is needed. We packed and made our way to the train station.

No laughter flowed from Bianca's throat during this visit. Her usually meticulous hair was in disarray and there were dark smudges under her eyes. Drago's body had been found in a field beside the railroad tracks. His tongue and nose were missing and part of his fingers. Bianca withdrew into her room shedding floods of tears; while her own life was likewise at risk.

By this time, I questioned whether anyone here was in charge of their life?

Not as long as war continues to be given a chance, was the reply.

On our way home, our train was derailed and I could understand what was meant by "sheer terror broke out" as people ran screaming, uncertain which direction to choose. We just kept moving with our eyes fixed straight ahead.

Eventually the tracks were cleared and we were fortunate to scramble onto another train that had arrived, while my child mind again failed to grasp what the lenses of my eyes had captured and there was no one to whom I could run for an explanation.

It was those in power who claimed to have the explanation, which could be enforced at gunpoint. When people walked along the sidewalks, they seemed to press themselves against the walls of the buildings in an attempt to be invisible, lest they draw attention.

"Probably, no nation is rich enough
to pay for both war and civilization.
We must make our choice;
we cannot have both."

ABRAHAM FLEXNER

THE ENEMY

If this is the lesson I had to learn then this is my story.
Pointing out how warfare effects and rules our lives.
Fighting for what they love by destroying others.

———————————— ⋙ ————————————

THIS quote I read somewhere, but don't know to whom it should be attributed.

The political situation took a rapid turn and clearly not in our favour. The Partisans now called each other comrades – a word they had adopted from the Russian Bolsheviks.

How does it feel to be the enemy? One thing became clear: the verdict came without a trial, and there was only one side that was laughing.

As I walked along the creek surrounding the spacious grounds of Berak, with Tatiana in my arm, the children from the hamlet unexpectedly showed up. At the head of them strode Helena with her head held high. With a smart salute as a gesture of her command, the children stopped in front of me, looking at me with eyes that suddenly seemed to belong to a group of strangers.

The shattering sounds of a reconnaissance plane abruptly dived down and all eyes looked skywards, then back down on me once the sounds zoomed into the distance.

"Svapski," (German) Helena indicated at the plane, studying my reaction. "Soon they will be gone, and there will be no one to protect you." Her eyes came to settle on Tatiana.

"Give me your doll," she abruptly demanded. "I want your doll!"

She held a branch with long, sharp thorns that she suddenly raised and drove into my arm while her eyes looked as hard as a pair of grey marbles, interlocked with mine. The pain was sharp and deep. Red droplets stained my skin. I could hear gasps from among the onlooking children, followed by nervous giggles. Instinctively I knew that nothing would ever be as it once was and there was no room for negotiation. Therefore, it seemed wise to obey her order.

She looked down at the doll in her arms, then back at me with a look of triumphant satisfaction. "You are no longer the princess daughter," she said.

"Your father is a dirty capitalist, and Svapski will no longer be tolerated around here! These are the orders from Comrade Tito."

She continued to glare at me and then called for Anica, at the back of the group, to step forward.

"Hit her," Helena commanded, as Anica stood in front of me.

Anica's eyes reflected a deep sadness as they looked into mine.

"You heard the order, comrade. Hit her!" There was a breeze ruffling Anica's hair; with our eyes still connected.

"Hit her!"

In that instant Anica's face changed to a blank expression as she likewise transformed into a stranger. Her body stiffened, her hand lifted and she slapped my face. For a moment, I could tell there was a stunned recognition – a shock of what she had done. Then she turned and walked away. Again, I asked, "Who is in charge here?" Clearly no one, as long as war is allowed to demand unquestionable allegiance.

And why do religions portray hell as being in some obscure, faraway place? As long as this kind of history is repeated, it could manifest right here in anybody's back or front yard.

In the meantime the stars and our planet we call home might alter its rotation and we mightn't even notice, because we prefer to remain oblivious in our slumber. Seasons come and go; new rivers carve their beds. But the strategy of warfare remains constant in tricking the mind into false perceptions. Destroy what we laboured over, while the soul is crying out in pain, unable to look on.

Jonathan

TOURISTS are taking each other's pictures in the square, kids are feeding the pigeons. Saul-Paul is sitting by the fountain with his face turned upwards in an offering to the sun.

"Good to run into you," he says as I take the seat beside him.

"Haven't seen you for a while," I say.

"Been hanging out in the Kooteneys," he said, while he sadly stared into space. "I am getting old, buddy. Just celebrated my thirtieth."

We hang out and listen to the band.

At dusk we head for the abandoned packing plant called "under the bridge." Saul-Paul says he has a surprise waiting for me. When we arrive, he shows me what he calls his secret room and we settle in for the night.

It's damp down here, and the door doesn't lock. Saul-Paul says not to worry, that we are protected. He tells me that he has received a message that he is meant to pass on and which he shares with me.

After a couple of nights, a rat attacks my toe sticking out of my sock. In the morning, I decide to leave. I call Mother at her workplace to pass on the message to her from Saul-Paul. She asks to meet her in Chinatown where we settle in the corner of a tucked away restaurant, where all eyes are directed toward the wall. Her old admirer friend Chuck is present, the one who said that "sometimes he looks totally normal," followed by a tap on his head... "and at other times, totally gone." I tell them I had met with Saul-Paul who had received a message and that I have found my purpose.

"And that is?" Chuck asks.

"I am a transmitter of the timeless source of information."

"And where does this information come from?"

"From the brain source of my Maker."

Chuck stares out of the window. Clearly, neither of them understands what I am saying, even though they pretend to. Instead of telling them the story, I move back under the bridge where I don't have to pretend to be who I am not.

Having arrived back down below, I pull my jacket over my head to shut out the day. The clanking sounds of car wheels are rolling above my head; they have a purpose. I have no car.

My father had a secret jar shaped like a fat pear. I'd never been able to open it. I think he kept my baby brain in it.

Somebody is shaking me and I realize that I must have fallen asleep. "Hey, wake up," a voice says.

It's Saul-Paul.

But I don't want to wake up. If I do, I will be forced to take part in this life."

Wake up," he repeats, "because you have to pass on the story."

"No, no more. Just let me go back to sleep, man!"

The story I am to pass on is how after he arrived in the Kootenays, while camped in the bush, Jesus told him "I appreciate your involvement, but understand that you are now also keeping me locked away and I need to be free."

With tears in his eyes, Saul-Paul added, "I loved him so much, I released him forever."

Back home, I look at this person who is my mother and see love in her eyes and sadness. A glance in the mirror reveals a young man who isn't as young as he used to be. I have passed my twenty-fifth birthday.

"What happened to the years in-between?" I ask. I decide to walk to the beach where I watch the silvery reflection on the water. Streams of laughter carry across to where I am sitting. I see couples everywhere, happy children and indulgent grandparents releasing kites, soaring in the air. Trees are nodding in the breeze. Birds synchronize their voices and all I want is to burst out of myself, but I am stuck.

I can feel myself drifting in and out of consciousness. My mouth snaps open, crying for my lost youth.

"How could you have interrupted what I am entitled to?" I scream, addressed at my Maker. "Gone, and where is the instruction manual? As for this life – I don't remember asking for it, which brings me back to the matter of choice. None!"

On the other hand, repeating Mother's words, I ask whether I maintain my state by feeding it.

Yesterday, as Mother and I walked along the inner harbour to watch the boat show, a gay pride parade was in progress. There was a guy wearing a leather motorcycle harness. He wasn't wearing anything underneath, however, leaving his ample rear end exposed and propped up by the leather ridge of the harness. Mother walked up to him and asked what this interesting contraption was called. "Chaps," he said.

She laughed, turned to me and said that one day we should organize a schizophrenic pride parade.

I like to see her laugh. Lately it seems to me that she is stepping over little barriers. I know it is she who passed on this condition but somehow she doesn't need to be fed the chemicals, as I do. Sometimes I get angry with her about this but she is slowly gaining in honesty and I appreciate her effort when she tries to meet me on my level.

Occasionally she takes me out for dinner to a restaurant, on a rating of the Empress Hotel dining room. I think this is to introduce me to an atmosphere of elegance in contrast to the atmosphere "under the bridge." Last time we dined here, I dropped my linen napkin and the waiter was right there to pick it up and whisk it away, but at the thought of spewing further unnecessary soapsuds into the environment, I asked him to hand it back for me to reuse. He started to rumble on about food safety, and I said, "Sir, there is a saying: The customer is always right," and Mother turned to look at him with an impish smile then winked at me and I liked her for that.

Then there was the incident when we saw the psychiatrist for another assessment of my condition and he found out that I hear voices, which he considered the ultimate sign of dysfunctionality, and Mother said she hears voices too. And he said, "That's not normal."

"For me it is," Mother said. "And for Jonathan it is."

"That's not normal," he repeated.

"For us it is," Mother repeated.

And his last words addressed to Mother were: "You are really stubborn, aren't you?"

"Thank you for the diagnoses," mother said, and that was the end of our visit there.

At other times I see nothing amusing in her humour because it's too much like everyone else's out there.

Leni

THERE IS BARELY
A CHANCE TO CATCH UP

THE seagull couple nestling on the roof are back from running their errands. Before Pau and I split up and he moved into a condo, he tried various ways to discourage them from nesting, but they continue to come back.

At their designated time, the eggs will crack. Usually, two or three fluffy grey balls emerge. Next, they practise balancing on their short legs under the supervision of the parents. At times they are visited by what might be an aunt or uncle, making a racket, perhaps debating over parenting skills. Eventually the chicks enter their gangly teenage period, pooping all over the roof and disrespectfully squatting over the gutters. The next thing to do is to coordinate their long skinny legs with their flapping wings before they finally graduate to lifting off the tiles. Occasionally, as today, one will fall over the edge of the roof.

I can tell by the parents' pacing and their urgent cries that they are attempting to encourage their young fledgling. But in the end when no rescue team is available, their efforts usually fail and their offspring ends up being devoured by the crows after all or by a crouching cat lying in ambush, a patchwork of feathers strewn across the lawn the sole evidence of the bird's short existence. As I look out of the front window, a flock of pigeons takes off from the tree in front of the house and then swoops to the sky.

Life ceaselessly churns and feeds indiscriminately on the type of mind-food that's served. At times, it races at such a speed there is hardly a chance to catch up. If there were a way, I visualize myself at intervals crawling back into the womb and giving me a break by folding the placenta around me.

"THERE IS NOTHING TO TALK ABOUT"

Introducing Pau

AFTER the completion of my immigration contract as a nanny, I applied for a position with a catering company in a mining camp on the north shore of Lake Athabasca, where the caribou crossed the frozen lake and the buffaloes thundered through the plains. That's where I met Pau – a tall handsome Spaniard with blue eyes and blond hair. One day in the early stages of our marriage, we went on an afternoon stroll on a visit in Toronto. As we were licking ice cream cones from an Italian deli across from a church, I said, "Let's go inside the church and absorb the silence."

I was surprised at his reaction. It was as if an eclipse had spread a shadow across his face. His pace increased so that I could hardly keep up.

"Is anything wrong?" I inquired.

"Don't ever ask me to go inside a church!"

When I encouraged him to talk about what to him seemed an issue, he snapped, "Why can't you leave things alone? Why do you have to dig into this psychological stuff? As I told you, there is nothing to talk about."

By then I had learned that where he couldn't go, there seemed little room for others to enter and that inside this athletically perfect body hid a vulnerability longing to be expressed, but not knowing how.

Perhaps it's those who shut out others and appear indifferent who ultimately turn out to be the most vulnerable of the lot. They might instinctively protect themselves from a past they are still unequipped to deal with. Whereas, from my perspective, undealt emotions distort the experience of the present and miss out on the magic in-between. Therefore, my own motto has become: "Dig, dig, lest these emotions manifest in illness, and that I must not overlook the invitation of the opportunities of lessons that arise. No matter how challenging they appear, invite them in. Maybe one day I will unravel the source of Pau's own untold story.

Jonathan

IF my Maker has made me the way I am does that mean I can't undo/outdo myself?

Must I unquestioningly accept myself as the creation that I am? How about when others won't accept me? In their image, they create me ... or re-create me, then. Either way that image then is not me any longer, nor is it them.

Who am I, once I am not me? Am I to be given a new name – their identity and not mine? Am I expected to live their experiences and not mine?

From somewhere a voice penetrates my brain: "Sorry buddy, we tried to make this work, but something broke in the process of the experiment; therefore, the odd piece somehow won't fit as it should. Mistakes are made at times, yet we think the experiment was worth the risk. You weren't quite right to begin with, although it could have worked."

At times, I am led into a torture chamber where the medical team tries to squeeze out memories that aren't there. This morning I awoke to a stillness settling in the room and my thoughts were connected in moments of remembrance. But now I can't remember what I was supposed to remember. A flash of lightning is crashing through my brain, splitting my thoughts. I can feel myself spinning and the sun is spinning with me. Then I come to an abrupt halt, like a driver suddenly slamming on the brakes. When I blink my eyes, I am standing at the edge of a cliff jutting out above the ocean and a voice is screaming from below: "He is crazy!"

Yes, I say to myself. And then I shout it out loud, "Yes! Yes, I am crazy!"

Next, I am suddenly flooded with a sense of elation. I know I don't have to excuse myself, nor do I have to pretend that I am anyone else. I'm free! I'm crazy!

What to do with this craziness? Should I hide it? Ignore it? Pretend it doesn't exist? Can I embrace it and dance with it? I am me – IAMTHATIAM!

Leni

THE WEEPING OF SOULS

*"We leave something of ourselves behind
when we leave a place; we stay there
even though we go away. And there are
things in us that we can find again only
by going back there."*

PASCAL

AS a Canadian National in the summer of 1966, for the first time, I felt safe to visit the country of my birth. I left Jonathan in Pau's care and picked up my new passport to board a plane to Austria. From there I rented a car to cross the border into Yugoslavia.

The country was still under the communist regime. My first impression was a state of drabness due to years of neglect. It was reflected in the clothes and the weary demeanour of its people. Even the buildings looked anaemic, sagging in resignation. The situation reminded me of the barefooted peasant women who were urged by the priest to uncomplainingly endure their lot because it would pave the road to heaven, he said. At the same time, the voices of this regime promised a collective earthly heaven of equality.

Plastered on the buildings were posters of euphoric workers carrying shovels, rakes, and pickaxes on their way to work. While on the other side of the continent, the message of capitalism urged: "Consume, consume," and later free trade was encouraged, which seemed the answer to global unification and prosperity.

I drove through the countryside in search of the landmark poplar trees that stood as silent sentinels guarding the entrance to the grounds of Berak. Soon I discovered the poplars had been cut for firewood, the house torn down and the bricks hauled away. In its place stood a cement building with a corrugated roof, typical of a communist collective farm; the ornate gate now a memory. I drove on to the little hamlet near the acacia grove where at sunset the shepherd used to play his flute and his flock lay at rest.

A few people stepped out as I parked the car, eyeing me curiously.

"Dobar Dan." Good day.

"Dobar Dan."

After I introduced myself, the news evidently spread, and others stepped out of their doorways. Some nodded, and shook my hand. One of them was an old man, who came up to join me.

I removed my shoes to make contact with the soil. Here, father would take me along on his rounds of inspection. My favourite time was when the sun sank into the horizon and the sky burst into pink and gold and the acacia trees released their sweet intoxication.

"I remember your father," the old man said. "He was a good man, and always generous to his workers."

He searched my face. "You used to come and play with the two little girls."

As I looked around, I recognized Anica's house and the outdoor oven and wondered how I would be received. The old man noticed and said, "They moved away." I felt sad as I realized that this was my main purpose in coming here – to re-connect with Anica.

As I silently gazed across the now neglected fields, an unsettling energy seeped from the ground, sending a chill up my spine. The ground I stood on felt as though it had a pulpy) consistency to it, like congealed blood. In my head, I could hear eerie sounds I imagined were the anguished weeping of souls. The old man looked at me with concern in his eyes. "Your face has suddenly turned a ghostly pale," he remarked. After I told him what I was experiencing, he looked at me steadily, without a hint of surprise.

His granddaughter came wandering over and snuggled against him. Sucking her thumb, she gazed up at this stranger standing beside her grandfather. He called her his "Dusa moja," which means "my little soul," and told me that in this field that we were standing on, with its feeling of pulpiness, a massacre had taken place towards the end of the war. Ruffling the child's hair, he said, "I couldn't bear for this little one to go through anything like that."

Little did we know then that like atrocities would be re-enacted almost thirty years later, what would manifest into the current Second Balkan War. I didn't ask what emblem the executioners on this spot championed. What was the point? The intent and retaliation would have been the same, no matter which side they were on, or what uniforms they wore.

A young woman, accompanied by a child, crossed the road. Alarm bells tingled at the back of my neck. I couldn't ignore those eyes with their intense expression. As they briefly connected with mine, I knew it was Helena. Then she turned and briskly walked away, while the old man silently watched the brief interchange.

Standing there, a wave of deep sadness and compassion swept through me as I grieved about the past dissensions that had swept away the laughter we once shared here.

When I took my leave, I braced myself for the next experience of reconnecting with our home from which we were expelled. On the way, I encountered a group of school children in their early teens. When they discovered I had arrived from Canada, I aroused their curiosity. I explained to them that I came to connect with the place of my birth. That here I was born into a Svapski (ethnic German) community.

They clearly didn't understand what I was talking about. "Of course not," I thought, "our history was obliterated from their countries records."

The middle-aged woman who answered the door after I introduced myself and asked for permission to refresh my memory was clearly familiar with our history and invited me in.

I looked around the peaceful courtyard where my Oma should have enjoyed her last days, my bridal pictures eternalized with a background of the oleander trees in mother's pretty pots, and the dragonflies hovering over the pond. Here my parents would have entertained their grandchildren and exchanged presents, with the tables lavishly laid with food grown on our land, had it not been for the war.

　　　　　　　　　　　　　　KATHARINA NOLLA

As I stood there, I was again overcome with deep sadness and compassion at the remembrance of those people who were my family, who had worked so hard and endured so much.

The paint was peeling, the tiles cracked, and the pond was no more; the oleander trees a faint memory. The woman apologetically explained that they had purchased the house from the party member it had been assigned to as a gift. This information came as no surprise as I thought of my Vukovar relatives. And via, the refugee grapevine, had spread the news of the 1950s Communist land reform program. During this reform, some 200,000 newcomers from other regions, colonists known as dosljaci (newcomers) had settled on our farms and towns in Eastern Slavonia. Jovica Stanisic's parents, who became the chief of Serbia's secret police, were dosljaci and Jovica grew up in one of these houses, built by ethnically cleansed Donauschwaben in the town of Backa Palanka.

The woman had kind eyes. "You don't have to apologize," I said, feeling a sisterly solidarity. "It was nice of you to let me look around. It meant a lot to me," and I spontaneously reached out to embrace her. It seemed that she understood. But I wondered what reception I would have received had the previous owners who had materially gained by our tragedy for a job well done still occupied the house?

The superpower administrations would not release any facts about these past conditions in Central Europe. There seemed to be a conspiracy of silence in the press pertaining to the Donauschwaben during the post-war period and have found little "relief" of any sort. They were never compensated for their property, nor given a chance to tell their story.

FINDING MY WAY

August 1992, Victoria, BC

I am walking my friend Thuy's dog along the beach. The tide is going out. The dog ventures down the rocks covered with seaweed still wet and slippery. On his way back up, he struggles on unsteady legs stiffly bracing themselves while I anxiously encourage him in his effort. Then I think just let him be and trust that he will find his way. And he does.

Arriving safely back on the path panting and shaking the water off his fur, he looks at me with soulful eyes. He enthusiastically wags his tail and rewards me with his slobbering tongue licking my hand then aiming for my face. I ask myself why do I trust him in finding his way, but don't apply this conviction to myself.

Faith: One must cultivate faith. It will pave the way to heaven, the church predicted. But no one could explain to me what faith was other than that one must have it. In catechism class the priest listed the myriad temptations the devil planted like land mines along the way, and in anticipation gleefully stoked the flames of his domain, ready to torture those who didn't have this conviction called faith. And one had to watch every move or not move at all. A reprieve was offered on Sundays, however, in the form of a wafer that represented Christ's body and melted away the accumulation of weekly sins.

There was a pre-requisite to this absolution. Agonizing hours of screening kept me awake the night before the communion lest any stragglers of unconfessed sins might be overlooked, hiding in the bushes of my mind. Ready to drag me down the pit of hellfire if I died before receiving the wafer of absolution melting under my tongue. The list of confessions had to be whispered into the priestly ear pressed against the latticed partition of the confessional, so close, I could see the bristles of hair sticking out of his ear. This unconfessed omission to the bristly ear weighed heavily on my mind, since everything on this level was monitored. The last words, whispered from the other side of the confessional each week, ended in the question "Did you do anything schweinisch?" (a colloquial word that translates as "piggish") referring to the unmentionable lower parts of the body, instigated by the devil waiting to claim those who did this schweinisch stuff. This insinuation clung to me like a sticky layer no bath could wash away.

How could I truly love God the way I was supposed to love, while bullets of disapproval pounded from the pulpit reminding me of my sinful nature? Only the saints were free of sin and, as far as I knew, they were all dead. This became evident by the line-up in front of the crypt that enshrined a saint's bones where candles were lit and donations dropped into a copper pot to earn special merit.

Adjacent to the crypt hung a painting of angels serenely playing their harps, while the sinners next door roasted in the fire. Ultimately, one had to give the angels credit for their frequent trips to purgatory to release the repentant souls.

I clearly needed all the help I could summon to release myself of this hereditary load and one day my child soul tapped into a silence immersed in light, inspired by a confidence that there was more than my eyes could see and that I merely had to recognize the opportunity when it presented itself.

It all started during one of my visits to our next-door neighbour, Frau Geber, who was a widow and whose two sons were still serving somewhere on the Russian front. Frau Geber had been to Amerika. She had little cards that magnified when placed behind a glass and that showed tall buildings, which were only to be found in Amerika, Frau Geber said. There were streets lined with cars that looked like boxes on wheels and men with their arms folded and legs crossed at the ankles, proudly leaning against these cars. There were pictures of a circus with lions and giraffes, and a lady with a beard. There were religious pictures with Jesus carrying the cross looking so sad, with blood running down his face.

She also had a book that showed photos of Hitler and his ministers and commandants, whatever they were called, Goebbels and Goering, Ribbentrop and Himmler. I would look at these photos and ask her why they were crying. She told me they weren't crying and I said, "Just look at their eyes, their eyes are crying."

She would simply smile at my comments and quietly continue with what she was doing – knitting socks for the soldiers at the Russian front whose feet were freezing. Intermittently she would pull out a box with the photographs of her sons, which she kept in a drawer, while through the silence the grandfather clock would impress its monotonous tick-tock sounds.

Then one day, at three in the afternoon, I drifted away to the sounds of the ticking and found myself in what

I can only describe as a vast cosmic cathedral, with light figures floating through this infinite peace of acceptance, immersed in a steaming pink bath. It was a place where I knew I would always be welcomed and never be judged.

When I returned, sliding back into the present, I found myself drowsily smiling at Frau Geber while she looked over the frame of her glasses and smiled back.

Later, after Tito gained power and we were declared the enemy, I saw Frau Geber's face float in and out among the crowd, as frightened and bewildered as the rest, and then I never saw her again, nor were her sons ever heard from. And who would continue to knit the socks for the soldiers?

As a survivor of such a system, I ask what I have learned from these experiences.

I have learned the importance of examining my own underground storage room or who else might have settled in there and ask if this is really the place where I want to be.

Acknowledge our pain before we can heal.

Be courageous, I tell myself, open your heart to yourself. Each time I discover another part of myself, I gain confidence in no longer having to seek approval in the eyes of others and indiscriminately follow blind orders. The privilege is in the seeding in the moment.

There was a time when humankind performed rituals to honour the gifts of nature, with the welfare of the present, but also with the future, generation in mind. It was an era they called the priestly time of the temples, with the soul recognized as the temple, and the body as the priest.

What is faith? It is the innate wisdom to trust my own voice that is calling, reminding me not to waste the privilege of the opportunities this planet has to teach me. Choose compassion and imagine what the other side likewise is going through, I remind myself, who are a reflection of myself. They, too have a story to tell and be sure to listen. "Aloha, Aloha." And rightly so, because this word translated into English, means I feel the breath of God in you. I am awed by the attention to detail the universe has invested in me: The spirals of my fingerprints, my irises and each toe, unlike any other. No brow matches mine; my navel differs from others. The way my hairline marks my forehead is uniquely designed for me. I am a miracle created with single-minded attention, having been issued with a passport to this life.

"Hallelujah!" translates as "Shine with God."

Jonathan

SCHIZOPHRENIA

WHAT is schizophrenia?

Schizophrenia is a road unmapped with no one to give directions along the way. I didn't choose this road. Who in their right mind would? I certainly wouldn't breathe life into something that hadn't been thoroughly pre-tested, I challenge my Maker.

Understand that each creation in its own way is a totality of completion," He replies.

"But I didn't ask for this kind of completion.".

There is only silence now.

"I tell you what," I add, "if this is supposed to be completion, then I gladly decline the offer. I even might place an ad: 'Schizophrenia: Free give-away, components spinning in perfect condition.' Then let's see how many replies I will get. It seems to me that I am caught in the middle of a story and who is telling the tale?"

"The universe is telling the tale, expressing itself through you."

"Let the universe entertain itself with someone else's story. By the way, what if I become trapped in this story? How long do I have to wait for my counter-story to begin? I might run out of time."

"Time does not run out, as you put it. All is motion and without you, the overall story wouldn't be complete – you being part of the motion."

"What if I ended this period right now?"

"You haven't signalled your consent. You see – you are fonder of Jonathan than you think."

"Thanks a lot, from now I will choose my own entertainment."

"As for the contract, life itself, is the contract," He continues.

"I don't remember signing a contract. But then again, I am always reminded that I don't remember."

"Aren't you curious about the ending of your story?"

"Should I be?"

BORDERS

CHURCHILL pushed the list to Stalin who made a large check mark on it with a blue pencil. Churchill then said, "Might it not be thought cynical if it seemed we had disposed of these issues, so fateful to millions of people, in such an offhand manner? Let us burn the paper." Churchill reports Stalin as saying: "No, you keep it."

During the early months of 1945 – before and after the war was declared over, borders were traps for displaced persons like mother and me. Two among millions of others, blocking the highways of war. It was a world where foreign soldiers from across the ocean, with rifles strapped across their shoulders, spoke a language that was incomprehensible to us and ours, to them. Unfamiliar with our history they made decisions that resulted in the loss of unaccountable lives – and these were no isolated stories.

Two months after the war, a dishevelled young woman appeared near the isolated farm house that mother and I lived in, with its scattered homesteads dotting the hillside. Whenever I attempted to make contact, she would scurry away to hide in the adjacent forest. One day I followed her. When she saw me, she cowered in fear. I placed a finger to my lips and said, "Don't be afraid, I can tell you are a Fluechtling (refugee) like me, I am not going to report you."

Her eyes widened in terror as she said, "If they find me, they will hand me back over to the Partisans, as they did before."

"Who are they, that would hand you over?"

"The English at Bleiburg."

By then, the mention of this Carinthian town at the Yugoslav–Austrian border, although a story censored to the world, had already evoked a sense of horror shivering through the refugee communication line.

Her eyes pleading with mine, she emphasized, "Then I would never have a chance to console my child's soul with beautiful flowers, nor burn a candle on her grave."

Her lips began to quiver as she raised her hands imploringly towards the sky, crying out, "Why didn't you take me instead?"

The wind rustled through the leaves, while I drifted into my own reverie as I thought of my Oma who had to be left behind.

"Because had He taken you instead," I reflected, "her innocent body would have been left to suffer at the hands of theirs – the Partisans," I said.

A gentle smile transformed her face. "Yes, she is now in His hands, isn't she, not theirs."

As young as I was, I knew she needed help but I had promised not to report her. Her name was Frau Driessen and throughout the following days, as I visited her in her hide-away she felt compelled to tell me the Bleiburg story.

It turned out that she and her child – like thousands of other civilians, mainly consisting of women and children and old men – had joined the vast columns of soldiers from the Independent State of Croatia on a massive exodus to surrender under British protection, in accordance with the Geneva Convention. It was over a week after the war was declared over. The British were stationed in the

Austrian border town of Bleiburg. The commanding officers of the Croatian Armed Forces led by General Herenčić established contact with the command of the British unit stationed there and told them that they wanted to surrender to the British Army and to put the 500,000 civilians under British protection to evade the massacre of the Partisans. The British commanding officer replied that he had been informed of the coming of the Croats, and that the Croats would be allowed to continue their march towards the West the following day and to keep their arms.

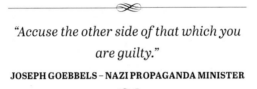

"Accuse the other side of that which you are guilty."

JOSEPH GOEBBELS – NAZI PROPAGANDA MINISTER

May 1945, Frau Driessen's story

After weeks of hardship, famished and traumatized, they arrived, spreading out across the field under the massive walls of Bleiburg castle with the assumption that some sort of shelter would be provided. After all, the occupying forces were a civilized nation, they told each other, and had been informed of their arrival. Among them were the moaning sick and wounded. Mothers tried to console their hungry, traumatized children wo failed to understand why they no longer had a bed to sleep in. The aged sat wringing their hands in despair as agonizing hours passed without food or water or the anticipated medical attention, Frau Driessen continued. While I wondered if the shivering little hearts were asking where the angels were that their mothers had asked them to pray to as every Catholic mother of that region would.

All eyes were fixed on General Herenčić who together with his interpreter conversed with the English brigadier by the name of Patrick Scott, gesticulating and speaking in a language not understood to the masses spread around. Night descended, rumours circulated. Further English personnel pulled up in jeeps, saluting each other and to the refugees' horror, among them appeared a Partisan general, Milan Basta, who seemed involved in the negotiation. Murmurs of prayers crossed a multitude of lips, buzzing an eerie sound through the chill of the night, a sound Frau Driessen knew would haunt her for the rest of her life.

After what seemed an eternity of debates and gesticulations among the occupiers and the way they eventually faced the hunched-over multitudes of bodies seemed to indicate that a decision had been reached. An interpreter appeared, addressing them first in Croatian, then in German.

After the final announcement, one collective wailing sound broke the stunned silence. She clutched her young child tightly to her chest and felt as if a bullet had already splintered her heart.

Undeterred by the desperate pleas from the field pointing out that mass slaughter and extermination camps were waiting for them on the other side, their supplication for surrender was refused.

At this point, rocking back and forth with her eyes staring ahead, Frau Driessen recalled what she described as the gates of hell opening, the sounds of machine guns popping from left and right as Basta's Partisans descended onto the meadow. Bodies collapsed like bowling pins. A man nearby dropped on his knees momentarily frozen as if in a praying position, clutching his intestines, which spilled out before he fell forward and lay still. According to a local eyewitness: "Soon so many people had been slaughtered that the Partisans ventured to descend among the survivors with bayonets" while the occupying forces remained silent.

Then began the enforced march back, which came to be called the Death March or the Way of the Cross.

Historical Report

The involuntary masses handed over to the Partisans and driven back across the border where the carnage continued, reflecting the tragedy of the so-called "Great Powers" dividing up the world and forcing hundreds of thousands seeking freedom to return to their captive nations against their will. It turned into an act of mass terror and brutal political surgery. The rest were subjected to abuse and long forced marches to extermination camps.

Further Footnotes

Russian Count and author Nikola Tolstoy reconstructed what happened when, on May 31st (21 days after the war) the commandant of the military camp at Viktring, reported that he had received orders for 2,700 of the civilian refugees in Major Barre's camp to be taken to Rosenbach and Bleiburg the following day, to be handed over to the Partisans. At this point I recalled the Cossacks performing their horseman acrobats and it was obvious that they would not have fared well with their communist adversaries – the Partisans, and the invading Russians.

The Lienz Cossacks as they were called were "white Russians," who had fought bitterly against Communism and the rise of the Soviet Union. The Lienz Cossacks sided with the Nazis in order to topple the communist regime and bring "freedom" to their country.

At the time of the Bleiburg repatriation, the British likewise rounded up the Cossacks. It was up to the United Kingdom to decide what to do with them.

Trains and trucks were pulled up and Cossack soldiers were forced into them. As were their wives, families and children – many of whom were not even Russian, having been born in Austria the years after the Lienz Cossacks had left Russia. The Cossacks didn't go willingly. British troops had to beat them into submission with riflebutts. It came to be called the betrayal of the Cossacks.

Eventually, almost 35,000 Cossacks were transported to their "mother country." The vast majority were immediately sent to labour camps in Siberia, which were little better than the death camps the Nazis had built.

No doubt all sides did their share of killing. After all, wars are not a matter about handing out roses, and even as a child I knew that Frau Geber did not knit socks for the Russian soldiers, nor did the Russian mothers serve tea to the German soldiers shivering in the freezing trenches.

Wars are no mere accidents, but strategically organized vendettas plotting against each other. Liberté, égalité and fraternité are merely concepts displayed on a flag that can be burned to ashes.

"We will have to repent in this generation not merely for the hateful words and actions of the bad but for the appalling silence of the good people. Human progress never rolls in on wheels of inevitability; it comes through the tireless efforts of men willing to be co-workers with God."

MARTIN LUTHER KING'S CALL

TO ACTION IS AS RELEVANT TODAY AS IT WAS IN

1963.

PLEASE, SOMEONE UNDERSTAND!

AN eyewitness, Jure Raguz, reported that in his vicinity before being handed over, he saw a desperate Croatian officer shoot his two small children, a boy and a girl, then his wife and in the end himself. The day after I read this report, this officer appeared to me in a dream. He was still a handsome man in his prime, clad in his uniform. His voice in the dream pleaded, "Please, someone, understand!"

Would it make a difference if I delved into the history of his past?

What can I say?

He was a soldier. No doubt a good soldier, who followed the orders as every good soldier must, no matter on which side. He was once the pride of his nation, surging forth on a fiery steed to do his country's bidding and to protect his family. The steeds had now turned to old hags dragging themselves to their death.

"Patriots always talk about dying for their country, and never of killing for their country."

BERTRAND RUSSELL

In war one side wins, the other is defeated. No doubt each side did their share of killing, it's what war is about, even though some might argue otherwise. At no time throughout these years of warfare, did the other side arrive with bouquet flowers, nor platters filled with cakes.

It would have been a lovely sight.

Why should further punishment have been added to an already tragic situation after the war was over and peace declared? Columns of the defeated soldiers who had also conscientiously served their nation, in humiliation were forced to shuffle towards appalling camps known for their high death rates and brutality. It seemed to me, that both sides should bond in solidarity and instead empathize with the unfortunate circumstances war had enforced on them. My child heart once more wondered what Jesus would say were he back. But patriotism and nationalism had replaced Jesus's true religion, while the collective soul called for liberation, and it was clear that both the perpetrators and the victims needed healing.

As long as wars are waged, there will be casualties and maimed survivors. For reasons, unknown, it was me and my family's turn to experience its impact this time around. It is not the kind of impact I wish on anyone. It's not the kind of life one has in mind for one's children.

Then why as a so-called 'civilized' species, do we continue to heed its call?

Some sides are alluding that warfare is a resolution that paves the path to peace.

I say, send food instead of bombs, and don't be afraid to turn to the light.

"YOU HAVE TO LISTEN!"

WHEN Frau Driessen told me the last phase of her story – the enforced march back to the other side – she covered her ears as if to drown out the screams of her memories. At that point, she said, she wondered if she were already dead and transported to hell as daemons unleashed their hatchets and thousands of bodies lay bleeding, clubbed to death with rifle butts, their throats slit, or fired at, close range.

This was not a movie with assigned actors playing their role, I told myself, as I covered my own ears and averted my face from her excruciating expression. My gesture clearly infuriated her, because she jumped up to attack me with her fists, screaming with rage and pulling at my hands.

"You can no longer look the other way and cover your ears, it's time to listen! The whole world needs to listen! Can't you hear the voices of their souls cry out?"

Then she roughly twisted my head to face her until I feared my neck would snap and I had to defend myself by running away.

The following day I returned with a blanket and spread it out. We lay down and absorbed the sounds of the rustling leaves and the silence of the trees, while she was able to cry and clearly felt compelled to go on with her story. And I listened.

THE WAY OF THE CROSS –
THE DEATH MARCH

ON the enforced march back her young child held on to her mother's skirt, whose hands were occupied, carrying their last necessities. The child failed to understand why her mother wouldn't provide any food or water. A high-pitched sound exploded inside the mother's head, and at her feet lay a small bleeding body. The child looked familiar, she then recognized it as her own. In desperation, she stuffed her kerchief into the wound and this seemed to reduce the flow. Summoning her strength, she picked up the body and ran while shots exploded around her.

When she entered the nearby forest, she sat down to rest. She noticed that her child's body had lost its warmth. She stripped off her clothes and laid the small form across her bare pulsating skin, then covered it with the same clothes.

It began to rain and she had to find shelter. Her only option was to take a chance to cross back over to Bleiberg once more, in the hope that this time she would not be sent back. The child was so quiet and wouldn't warm up.

When she arrived on the other side, an English soldier stopped her, pointing his rifle at her. She pleaded to take her child to the hospital. "Ausweiss," (identification) he said in broken German. – He was clearly another good soldier following the right orders. Terrified, she shook her head. She had no Ausweiss! He pointed to the other side of the border.

"Nein," she screamed, "nein!"

They took her child away. A man who spoke German arrived. He looked familiar; she had clearly seen him before. "Ich bin der Burgermeister" (I am the mayor) he said, whom she now recognized as having taken part in the previous negotiation. All she could think of was her child and that she might be sent back and separated from her. The Burgermeister began arguing with the soldier in a language she didn't understand. She was so exhausted the world began to spin and she passed out.

When she revived, it was night. It seemed to her that everything was always happening during the chill of the night. An Austrian nurse was bending over her. She had kind eyes. But all that was on Frau Driessen's mind was "Mein Kind!" (My child!)

The nurse placed a finger over her lips. She explained as gently as possible that her child was now safely resting in God's arms, and that both the child and God would want her to save herself. She handed her a little package of food and asked her to follow because if she didn't, the occupation would likely send her back as they had others.

But the child had to be properly buried with a priest to give the last rites, and the grave marked with a cross. The nurse promised that she would fulfil her wish. She said that once Frau Driessen felt safe to return, she could come back and lay beautiful flowers on her child's grave. At the mention of the flowers, she paused, and for a moment a heartbreaking little smile played on her lips. "Yes, beautiful flowers," she said.

My thoughts settled on the officer who had shot his family, and I understood it was his way of saving them from a fate worse than any imaginable hell.

Eventually I managed to convince Frau Driessen to come out of hiding and suggested that together we pay a visit to the local Burgermeister in the adjacent town who would know what to do and maybe get her an Ausweiss.

After our visit to the Buergermeister we embraced and that was the last I saw or heard of her, but I was convinced that she made it back to Bleiburg, guided by her new Ausweiss and God's protection, arriving with a candle and a bouquet of flowers to console her child's soul.

In the meantime, further news circulated from across the border that it was safe for us to return. Picturing the peaceful courtyard with its pond and the oleander trees waiting in their pretty pots, the lace curtains swaying in the breeze, the silverware in the drawer and the china in the cupboard, mother was ready to pack up to escape our miserable squalor. But soon evidence from the shell-shocked escapees proved otherwise. We heard our neighbor Frau Geber was one among those who had chosen to believe the promises, because here she imagined that's where her sons returning after their battle at the Russian front, would be looking for her. Instead she soon found out that the call back was a deception and managed to join the Bleiburg march headed for Austria. Only to be recognized by a survivor, seen lying in a pool of blood. A photo of her sons lay under her dead hand. At the same time, the skeletal photos of Hitler's concentration camp survivors circulated shock waves throughout the world. Endless columns of captured Wehrmacht soldiers, trudged towards Siberian camps known for their brutality and short lifespan to pay the price for their defeat, whose Fuehrer had decided to check out.

While in another part of the world, scorched bodies stumbled through the streets and collapsed under the heat of an ominous mushroom cloud. Death claimed 140,000 lives in a city called Hiroshima and in another, called Nagasaki.

I eventually managed to convince Frau Driessen to come out of hiding and suggested that together we pay a visit to the local Buergermeister in the adjacent town who would know what to do and maybe get her an Ausweiss. After our visit to the Buergermeister we embraced and that was the last I saw or heard of her, but I was convinced that she made it back to Bleiburg, guided by her new Ausweiss and God's protection, arriving with a candle and a bouquet of flowers to console her child's soul.

War is a rapist driven by a lust for power. In certain circles of governing it is viewed as shock and awe accompanied by impressive displays of fireworks, and waving flags of patriotic glory. Thousands of children die as a result of sanctified starvation, and by some is declared worth the price as the solution.

It is an unrestrained rage where the police should be called to intervene. But in war no intervening brigade is available. Rather, it is about eradicating other minded people, claiming it is heroic to blast them out of the way.

Occasionally one nation awakened to a momentary state of consciousness and in righteous indignation took action against those they accused of war crimes by targeting civilians – particularly against children. Retaliating by abusing their own military power to indiscriminately kill additional children in place of negotiation.

After the news of our dear neighbour Frau Geber's death, I was haunted by nightmares and bolted out of my sleep in which I vicariously experienced her fate mother and I had been spared. My body suffered to a point of depletion where I began to faint and considered consulting the local doctor. But doctors charged money and I had no money.

One day I dared to knock on his door.

The nurse let me in, he kindly listened. In the end, he concluded that I suffered from survivor's guilt that compelled me to internalize Frau Geber's experience.

I recalled grandmother's mentioning the curse, and Ivanka's opinion that finding the right magic is the only way to cure a curse. If warfare is mankind's self-inflicted curse, what is the magic?

The doctor further explained to me how our collective traumas have a generational impact, and the healing process will take time.

"How long?" I asked.

He looked deeply into my eyes then said slowly, "At least three generations."

Now many years later as wartime post-traumatic stress syndrome is becoming recognized, and the sexual abuse of First Nations residential schools made public, I recall the doctor's answer, and Frau Driessen's words: "You listen. Do you hear, you can no longer look the other way, it's time to listen!"

As I am ruminating on this past, the story told to me by a native man, comes to mind: The missionaries wanted to translate 'the bible into the native language.

"Tell us, what is the equivalent of 'sin' in your language," they asked. The Indians didn't have a word for sin. They considered their children sacred and said: "Our children are our future, and when you shatter those lives, the lives of the children, then you shatter our future. That's the sin.

In my dream that night I was shown a symbol that when I searched the Internet, showed up as the Endless Buddhist Knot. The symbol of intertwining lines represents how all phenomena are conjoined and yoked together as a closed cycle of cause and effect.

Endless Buddhist Knot

After this revelation, I woke to the realization that I am a conscious being and at this insight I wanted to turn around and go back to sleep. I tried to remember what day of the week it was but the answer eluded me. All I knew was that I was conscious, encompassing my pain and that of others' and the inflicted suffering of warfare desperately wanting to be acknowledged. When I approached my brain, demanding an explanation, it frantically rummaged through its filing cabinet, while my cells begged for a chance to rest.

...Rest.

Rest and know that IAM THAT I AM

KATHARINA NOLLA

ARRIVING AT THE CROSS ROAD

"Those who cannot remember the past
are condemned to repeat it."

GEORGE SANTAYANA

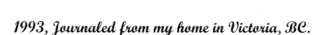

1993, Journaled from my home in Victoria, BC.
A memory dated back to age fourteen

IF you feel hatred welling up, don't deny the feelings that arise. Examine the lessons which need to be learned instead, is my advice.

Leni's advice

One day on my solitary one-hour walk home from school at age fourteen, I was suddenly overcome with a surge of heat rushing through my veins so intense it threatened to consume me. I found myself raging at everything this war had imposed on me and on others, including my worn-out shoes and threadbare dress. The humiliating subsidized post-war can of spam I picked up on the way home, replaced the abundance of our pantries stacked with the food of our land and our livestock.

Where had they disappeared to?" I seethed. Those who had ruled our lives and had packed up their promises and crept away, having left others to clean up the mess and cope with the devastation.

Just as my jaw for the second time threatened to snap off its hinges, ready for a raging scream, I recognized what I was experiencing.

It was a delayed reaction, fuelled by the impact of hate, which had shown up to recruit me in its ranks. I realized that I stood at a crossroad, where I was forced to choose the outcome of my destiny: Tempted by a belated urge that felt sweet and enticing to impose suffering on those who had imposed it on me. Next, a drawn-out scream burst from my throat and reverberated through the fields: "No, no-o-o-o-o!" It was my own voice calling out.

From that moment on, how could I judge those who snap from the overload and choose a different direction from mine? What can I say? Am I further evolved than the next, more civilized? Most of us can claim to be civilized before the muck rains down on us. And some might lack the strength to dig themselves out.

On the other hand, I could have chosen to ignore these emerging outbursts and looked the other way and justified my reaction. In the long run, however, it seemed wiser to deal with that rage, I decided, lest it manifest in illness, or drag its ammunition into the future.

Throughout my months of journaling, I have become a pretty good editor, having learned to edit out part of my inner chatter and to relieve my brain of its overload.

Another memory emerged: My early childhood ritual by laying my clothes out in the right order to slip on, instructed not to wait for anyone in case of a nightly raid. I had to train myself to be strong and detach myself from my family and from life itself because any night could result in permanent separation. Something was missing. I had lost part of myself ... one day I might be able to cry.

In Catholic paintings, the grieving part was assigned to mother Mary, the eternal queen of suffering portrayed shedding tears of sorrow, grieving for her children who can't get along with one another.

"What we do in life echoes in eternity"

MAXIMUS IN "THE GLADIATOR"

During a subsequent meditation, I found myself standing in the desert facing the Burning Bush depicted in the bible, with the legendary voice saying, "Take off your sandals, for the ground you are standing on is holy ground." Of course, I thought to myself, all ground is holy, created from the divine source of light and energy. Even the ground where the enforced repatriation massacre took place – the blood-soaked ground adjacent to the hamlet of Berak – all is holy and should not be defiled.

Shouldn't the nuns and priests who regressed to child molestation in the Residential schools have known that the ground they were standing on was holy? Created from the eternal source? Of course, I must not forget that the ground I am standing on is likewise holy. The mind is holy ground, which should not be defiled by lashing out in anger. I could live in blissful denial by overlooking my own trespasses along the way, but in the long term I cannot walk away from myself. It will merely follow me as my shadow, reflecting my internal self.

"Oh God, how can I be of service?" I cried out.

"Are you prepared to enter into the sacred?" a soundless voice asked. What is considered "the sacred?" I wondered, puzzled by this question. In answer, I was shown images of enforced prostitution, the underground corruption that leads to violence, the ugly face of greed and the brutality of war.

"How could what I was shown be categorized as sacred?" I asked.

"That's where primary help is needed and healing is invited to take place," was the answer, "and once you step aside beyond your self-imposed complacency, you will be able to assist others."

Am I up to this task? I wondered.

All I could reply is that I am willing to prepare myself. With full awareness that a great amount of clearing lies ahead and for that, I have to examine my own emotions standing in the way of progress.

FEAR

"I want to know God's thoughts ...
the rest is details."

ALBERT EINSTEIN

FEAR is one among the record keepers of my emotions that, when shut away in a chamber of denial, can turn into a sneaky companion, creating havoc in my overactive imagination. Rummaging through my mind like a restless ghost, provoking my adrenalin into action.

Having struggled through periods of depression in search of myself, it became clear what was missing – I hadn't allowed myself to grieve.

After all, this is not a planet for the weak. I had a child to support after Pau and I split up and I had to become the sole provider. I had locked myself into my insecurities that traumatized my cells. It is time to reclaim their radiance, the mystery beneath all forms.

"Hello Fear," I call. I am surprised by a presence of serenity as if I had found a friend, one I could confide in. Now why would fear feel like a friend?

Next, I find myself immersed in a kaleidoscope of pink and blue colours. I see a bridge leading to the other side from where I am standing. Through the mist of colours, I see God's face smiling down, saying in a wordless voice, "Welcome to the great mystery."

What is this mystery?" I ask.

As no answer is forthcoming, I repeat my salutation: "Hello Fear."

Again I am surrounded by calmness and I come to understand that as a record keeper, Fear had "seen it all" and is familiar with the multiple personalities with which the human mind struggles. Some of these established personalities hang on more tenaciously than others and death at times can be a long, drawn-out process.

Light-swirls of energy dance around me. On the other side of the bridge, a landscape like a Matisse painting shrouded in a veil of mist is enticing me to cross.

What is Fear trying to show me?

"Come," it says.

Dejected bodies looking like variations of a black and white Munch print, "The Scream," shuffle through the landscape. At the sight of them, I am overcome with compassion. There is great suffering here and I understand why God's face has appeared amidst it all.

"Do they represent the terror of our disconnectedness?" I ask.

Fear's eyes express the confirmation.

"This is the mystery," it tells me "Shoving me out of the way is not the solution. Remember the saying that 'what you resist, persists?' Embrace me, and honour me for what I am.

"I am glad I asked," I say, and I come to understand that by crossing this bridge, Fear is teaching me its valuable lesson of compassion. "Cross the bridge often in order to assist others, for this will help you understand yourself."

Jonathan

YESTERDAY when I stepped outside, angry clouds chased each other across the sky. The street looked like a grey tunnel with the wind racing through, claiming any unattached object in its way. I jumped and snatched what I thought to be a red disk from its clutches, hurled towards my face. As I did so, a vision of Botticelli's golden Venus rose from the sidewalk, saying, "That's my hat, thank you for rescuing it." Before she walked away, she smiled at me and then disappeared into the restaurant not far away.

Now a day later, sitting in front of the old post office with a view of the restaurant, I clutch the wrapped box that I want to present to her. Shortly, I see her walk in my direction. In passing, I inhale her perfume trailing through the air, and the world feels wonderful. I get up to follow her. "This is for you." I say, holding out the box with its golden ribbons. "I painted it." But she merely increases her pace, her back as rigid as a tank. I suddenly feel under attack. A shower of rocks pelts down, reptiles slither in my direction, cackling and flicking their tongues. I fling the present into the traffic. In a movie, I saw recently, the main character was a slave shackled to his chains. The battle cry of his pent-up anger became the fuel that cracked those chains. I am that slave!

Next, I run into the sports store nearby. I pick up a baseball bat then run back out, swinging it in all directions to ward off the rocks and the cackling reptiles, screaming at them to get out of my way!

In the back of my head I hear the police siren and I know when to run, and where to hide under the bridge. Night settles under the bridge. I try to drift off to a space that is exempt from participation. Just as I doze off, I am jarred back by a presence bending over me. A voice penetrates my brain. My chest tightens, forcing out a cough.

"It's me – your mother, Jonathan."

I blink some more – it's mother. She seems to have this knack for sniffing me out. I notice that she is decked out in her pearls, saying something about a concert and the news broadcast, and that she was worried I might be down here. She's asking me about a stabbing or a suicide or something like that.

"I don't know anything," I say. "I just want to be left alone."

I think she tells me that I need to see a doctor, that she is worried about my cough. As if it matters. I am fully awake now. There is no escape from the deception. Everywhere I look there are ads about playfulness, promises of togetherness.

"Why did you have to pass it on?" I ask her.

"Pass what on?"

"This fucking condition, you passed it on!" Next, I catch myself screaming. But when I stop, I can't remember what I was screaming about. I think she is crying. I am sorry I screamed at her. I tell her that one day I will live the counter-story for her.

Next, everything is a black void. And then, there is life in the void and I know it's him, Lucifer, who once shone brightly than any star.

"You are becoming like me," he says, "another fallen star." He thinks his comment is so funny that he doubles over laughing.

"I don't care! I just want to be left alone!"

"Too late," he winks as he looks over his shoulder. Then I find myself surrounded by dozens of them, all in his likeness, clapping, and banging on tinny drums. I place my hands over my ears and scream.

"Do I detect that perhaps you don't like it here?" he taunts. "You don't care to stay with your mother; the place under the bridge is going to be demolished. You will sooner rather than later be faced with a choice."

At this, the entire assembly howls with laughter, banging their drums.

"But there is a secret to this," he says, after they exhaust themselves laughing. "The secret is that you have chosen already. After all is said and done, you are the catalyst of your destiny."

"No," I scream. "You are trying to trick me. I had nothing to do with this!"

The sounds continue, clanking and crashing and hooting all around me with renewed intensity. I want to run but I can't. I'm stuck in this infernal cacophony. Then I realize what I am experiencing: I am experiencing my own suicide. My muscles tighten and scream in terror, my adrenals activate their reserve.

Next, I find myself in a space of stark whiteness, with a feeling of nausea surging through my body. They bring in mother, who is crying. I am fascinated by her limp white hands, which are dangling like a pair of captured doves below her belly. Then I realize they are snapped together with handcuffs. "Here she is," a voice says, "she who passed this on." All eyes are fixed on me, waiting, but I don't know what's expected of me.

A man walks in. "Let's get this show on the road," he says, and hands me a judge's robe. Again everyone waits with their eyes fixed on me, including mother, with her hands still bound.

"Well," the man says, "what is to be done with her?"

"Just leave her out of this!" I scream.

Accompanied by a clucking sound, the man shakes his head. "You accused her of having passed this on, now tell us what you want done with her."

"Let her be!"

Suddenly the lights are dimmed.

Next, a nurse bends over me, tightening a blood pressure cuff on my arm. Mother is standing at the end of the bed. I look at her bound hands. They are freed, and holding a bouquet of flowers. In a flash, I remember. "I saw Lucifer in his scorched state."

She looks at me sadly.

One of my legs is elevated, hanging in the air, with bandages wrapped around it and a voice says, "To have been torn and splintered, to have wrenched the unresolved from its depth to be examined – that is art."

"I am no fucking piece of art. And I don't want to be used as an experiment," I scream.

I recall a lance pursuing me through my dream, swishing through the air with rapid movements, pointed at my chest. At one point, I was tempted to bare myself to its thrust and be done with it. "The symbol of piercing your chest means the desire to awaken to life," the previous voice is saying.

Leni

A few days ago, I saw Jonathan bent over a canvas, cheerfully squeezing blobs of paint onto a palette with a sweet smile playing on his lips, completely absorbed in the glow of the colours. He mumbled something about it having to be the right shade of gold. When I tried to peek, he turned in a way that prevented me from seeing his work. But I walked away singing inside, pleased that he had taken an interest in his art again.

Now, back from a visit at the hospital, standing on a cliff overlooking the ocean, I try to understand what could have so suddenly altered my son's mood.

The sea appears calm and satiny. The sun is climaxing in its finale, dispersing its rays to dance on the stage of the ocean, casting a pink glow over the snow-capped mountains, lined in a row across the water. Then as if by the flick of a magic wand, the sun transforms into a golden disk hovering deliberately before submerging, inch by inch, into the curve of the horizon, finally coming to rest beneath the feet of the mountains. Jewels of light begin to blink across the water. It feels as though evening is holding its breath in awe, while my heart fills with compassion. I feel kinship with all beings of creation and pray for those unable to perceive its sacredness.

My mind turns back to recapture the moment when I pulled out of the parking lot with the radio turned on. A dead body had been found in the abandoned packing plant locally referred to as "under the bridge," it announced, jolting me from my tranquil mood after attending a concert. I immediately thought of Jonathan. That's where he hangs out at times and he hadn't been around for three days.

"Please let it not be Jonathan," I prayed. No, it can't be him, he hasn't had a chance to live life fully yet. I raced through the streets until the bridge loomed ahead. A harsh wind whipped the shrubs as I stumbled down the bank wrapped in darkness. Halfway down, I tripped and hit the ground with my heel caught in a coil of wires. I managed to retrieve the damaged shoe and stumble down.

Down below, the space was shrouded in grey obscurity. Ghosts of mould had settled on the walls, oozing a chilling dampness; my leg began to throb with pain. The only illumination that penetrates this habitation is weak threads of city lights, reflecting off the water. Grey shadows paced in agitation. I found my son wrapped in a threadbare sleeping bag, lying on the floor.

Next, the place was flooded with lights, awakening to a confusion of running feet and cursing voices. Invading uniforms took charge. I saw Jonathan jump and rush up to the bridge. So did I.

Seconds later, he had disappeared.

"He jumped!" I screamed.

Jonathan

THE medical team keep saying it's a miracle I'm alive. Is a good day really a good day and a miracle really a miracle? Threads of thoughts wind through my brain without pause. I can't sleep. I try to chuck out what emerges but whatever I discard re-emerges. "What is this," I scream, directed at my Maker. "Am I someone's recycling bin?"

"My own recycling bin?"

"Show me your face," I say to my Maker.

"You know my face. Whatever face you give me, that is it."

Now that they've stopped telling me I am a miracle they keep asking why I jumped. And then why can't I remember that I jumped? How can I explain why I can't remember what I am to remember? I can see Mother is upset. She's always upset when I don't remember.

Next, I recall the heavy impact on my body as it hit the ground, then lifted on a stretcher, a voice say, "Close call!"

I feel a presence close by.

It's death.

I engage Death, who always hovers close by in such situations, in dialogue, wondering if it was the time to take me away?

Death: "I am not the decision-maker," Death explains, "but arrive at your moment of surrender to wrap you in my mantle and show you the sites of rest. The condition some of you arrive makes me weep. It seems that once you arrive on this earth plane, you become obsessed with writing your mental scripts. Oh dear, oh dear, such busy scribes have you become, arguing over the direction of your play and the rights to production. No wonder you are confused, so pre-occupied are you with your script that you forget your life's purpose. It seems as though you have drawn a ticket but don't know whose ticket you drew. Could it have been the clown at the corner of the square who winked at you and held out his hat saying, "This is a lottery, dive in to pick your ticket, then mix it with the others and at the end of the day you might win a prize." The tricksters show up in many places and the truth is to some of you, life appears more frightening to you than I, because ultimately I provide a state of rest, whereas life does not allow you this but spins and churns and the lights never seem to switch off."

I hear something click from the vault of my storage room. It's mother's voice from the past speaking to my father. "It's all recorded inside of you; you just don't want to go there, but rather let it pile up until it drowns you!" I was a little kid then and I have a flashback of he and I passing a church one day. The door was open wide so we walked in. Looking around, he frowned then his eyes briefly settled on the statue of Jesus. He seemed far away. He said words in Catalan I didn't understand. At times he called me "chiquet" – which in Catalan means kid. "What did you say?" I asked. When he looked down, he seemed surprised that I was there, andhe said it means hijacked and locked away. His eyes strayed once more, then came back to settle on mine. "Never let anyone take your power away, hombre." That's what he called me when he included me in his manly talk. Then we walked back out. Among all the words that have been said, now obscured in a fog, these always seem to stand out. "Blow the world a kiss and dance," a voice said.

"Sure, sure," I mimic in reply.

No virus found in this message.

Leni

MOTHERHOOD

"Without contraries is no progression."

WILLIAM BLAKE

MY friends will remind me to give myself a break when they see me pace with my mother-guilt cradled in my arms, robbing me of my blessings.

Self-deprivation feels like a dead space where I never measure up, as I should; where guilt props up the entire structure to keep it alive. That is so big and I so small. It is an addiction that can become a cult that smacks of virtue, with its antennae busily scanning, asking, "Are you there? Are you there?" And as long as it feels supported, it continues to hang around,

This is not a particularly easy journey, with its past programming keeping a vigilant watch so as not to be upstaged by other views keeping me hostage to its demands. They insist, "I was here first," as if Orwell's Big Brother were standing over me. I used to spend hours ruminating, "maybe this would help, or that," licking my self-inflicted wounds. I pelted myself with recriminations for having failed to recognize Jonathan's early symptoms, which might have shed some clarity on the situation and driven me to search for alternative interventions. The moment you become a mother, you are hooked. You are handed this precious little miracle that is part of yourself and no matter how life turns out, you will share its joy and absorb its pain. A mother's happiness is gauged by the degree of her child's happiness.

Again I ask, "Am I to blame for Jonathan's condition due to neglect?" Then I have a sudden flash of insight into what Jonathan means by promising one day to live the counter-story for me. The counter-story in this case would be the perfect life as we conceptualize it, polished back to its original lustre as I imagine it once was. What if there were a program designed to drag the cursor of my personal history back to the beginning of time, then again forward to the present – on its way back deleting the accumulated pile-ups of the out-dated perceptions, edited out. It would include my perception I see as failed opportunities erased and my self-blame of the "done and should-not-have done," removed.

…It would clear the path for fresh opportunities to jump in, clad in renewed confidence, smiling encouragement. Entering an unobstructed glorious future that is already beckoning on the horizon.

*"Remember, I feel that we are right now &
thinking, talking, walking, and
manifesting, our way into a new
tomorrow!"*

MARY ELIZABETH THUNDER

I have become too complex for my own comfort. Although I know better, I do not always act according to my advice. An announcement from my inner voice says: "She who can't accept herself is a fool, generating acres of regrets that choke out life. But those who get to know themselves will not be deceived, because you can't sell them what is counter to their personality. And don't rely on the thinking mind to rehash its thoughts. Become aware of your awareness. Again, my advice is to "go home and have a good relationship with yourself."

Jonathan's way of thinking is a consequence of his brain chemistry, I was told. On the other hand, maybe it is the other way around – the chemicals are a result of his thinking. When his words echo back: "Why did you pass this on?" I think perhaps there should be a warning posted for those waiting in line to sign up for their prospective womb serving as a conduit to this planet earth experience.

DON'T SIGN UP WITHOUT CHECKING ITS REFERENCES!

When the Ego Sneaks in

*"Do not imitate the way of this world
But be transformed by the renewing of
your mind."*

ROMANS 12:2

SOMETIMES my friend Ida and I are too busy to meet. There is one mutual ritual we never break, however, and that is the annual attendance of the pre-Christmas concert of Handel's Messiah.

Ida says she can tell when I drift into a state of trance. It is a state when I absorb the sounds through the base of my skull instead of through my ears. At that moment, I become the sound itself, floating along the ceiling with kundalini blisses snaking up my spine.

There is another side to this experience. When I step out, and I observe myself pointing: "Look what I can do!" Because once I experience this kind of bliss, I crave for more, while my ego-self continues to demand a large share of acknowledgment. It fails to recognize that when you are invited, you must learn to understand the rules and what you try to possess will elude you. It's like trying to capture the graceful beauty of a butterfly, thereby stifling its spirit you so admired. And when the angels are in the mood to play, any interference will dispel the moment.

Or I lose direction and become distracted by the past or agonize over the future, while the present is unable to understand why no one wants to play with it, or is in the mood to share its blessings.

At times Ida and I laugh and joke that whoever will be the first to depart into the beyond must promise to return for our traditional rendezvous at the concert. And be sure to be punctual, so that we can enter together.

PART II

In Search of Myself

MENTAL CLOSETS

Projection from the Human Psyche

*"Our physical body possesses a wisdom
which we who inhabit the body lack.
We give it orders which make
no sense."*

HENRY MILLER

I am waiting to board the Saturna ferry on my way to my cottage. When life seems to race off track and I am pulled into the vortex of my complexities, I go for a reality check to spend time in nature's hideaway of simplicity. The sun is shining and I am sipping my Kicking Horse coffee, allowing my mind to shift to autopilot. An announcement echoes through the loudspeaker. A man wearing the familiar yellow-striped vest with the logo of BC Ferry is tapping on my car window, asking to see my ticket. I hand it over. He looks at it and says, "You are in the wrong lane."

I smile and point to the Saturna sign on my dashboard, although a sliver of my mind wondered why the ticket clerk pointed at lane 33. The Saturna lane is forty-two.

"You have to go back to exchange your ticket," the man says, and I realize the announcement had been for me. As I look at the various lanes, my head is spinning, my stress level escalating. "If I go back, I might take a wrong turn and miss the ferry," I say.

I can hear the reply from the other end. "I am afraid there is no other way. If she doesn't come back now, she will definitely miss the ferry."

I turn on the ignition and race back to the ticket booth. It seems that part of this confusion is a matter of a $2.45 price difference between the Saltspring and Saturna fare. I pay and race back. My lane is empty; anxiety takes over. Another man in a yellow-striped vest waves me on.

"Saturna," I say frantically. He has a friendly smile. "You'll make it," he says. "Just follow the white truck."

When I turn the ignition off and relax into my seat, I think, Wow, what was this all about? What a force I must be to be reckoned with in my insecure spin! I drift into my silence.

"Remember to always stay together," a voice whispers, directed from the past. "If you become separated, no one will be able to wait for you."

So much for escaping into simplicity I looked forward to. But from experience I have learned not to dismiss the clues that arise, since they invariably have something to tell me.

And so, they do.

These words from the past trigger a memory taking me back to the night when a group of us were waiting for the stars and the moon to go into hiding. The whirling snowflakes are thick and heavy, obscuring our vision. Our aim is to cross the border into Hungary from where to reach the safety of Austria. Guards are patrolling the border. I am worried about my Oma who was left behind who I was told had been too weak to make the trip for now.

Once we are on our way, it's so dark and I badly need to pee, to the point where I can't control the urge any longer. I move out of line and pull down my underwear underneath the bulky layers of winter garments. No one seems to notice and after I am done, I can no longer see the others.

Where are they?

Which direction do I take?

Panic! They can't wait, but have to move on. I am scared, but did not cry out. If I had, the entire group would be endangered – so we were warned.

Tears flow down my cheeks, blurring what little vision there is. I stumble on then lose balance; my mouth fills with snow. I manage to pull myself up only to sink deeper, with each step. As I struggle on, a light illuminates the way. I can see the footprints the others have paved. The light reflects from an apparition clad in a white gown, a halo shining bright and gentle, floating alongside me, guiding my way. Evidently no one else can see him. I know it's Jesus. Then the group of people are looking my way, mother's lips are mouthing, "Gott sei dank, Gott sei dank!" (Thank you, God.)

Amazing, how my present reaction has provided the detective work to trace back to that past experience thereby explaining another aspect of my life, in search of myself. This memory also clarified my resistance to organized tours. I am fine when I travel alone and getting lost can be seen as an adventure of new discoveries. But being confined to a group designated to meet at a particular location invariably stirs up the familiar feelings of anxiety.

Back in the present, the hull of the ferry unhurriedly slices through the calm waters of the Georgia Strait, while on shore, the homes and cottages placidly gaze out at the sea and I drift into a meditative reverie. I am awed by the capacity of data my brain is capable in storing until such time as I am ready to sort through and deal with it.

At times I behave like a compulsive housekeeper, sorting out the clutter. No sooner am I done with sorting one corner, then the next calls for attention. And it is I who has to do the job. No one else knows what's stacked inside my mental closets.

I watched a film on dolphins, elegantly gliding in synchronized rhythm, caressing each other and making joyful cooing sounds. They make excellent parents who pay full attention to their babies. If re-incarnation is in the plan, then I want to be a dolphin mother the next time around. No housework on the agenda, no cooking or shopping distractions, nor real estate demanding its share of maintenance – I would have all the time to devote to my babies.

How about Adam and Eve? Did they devote their time to housework in the Garden or was it an affair of open-air living, with an automatic cleaning system that rained down from heaven to do the job? Did they cook their food or did they live on fruit, nuts and seeds, spending unlimited time with their babies?

When did the idyll turn dysfunctional? "And Cain killed Abel." Ironically, the first homicide according to this history was committed to please God, that had compelled the brothers to compete for his favour. But hadn't God made something clear already when he announced on the seventh day as He looked around, smiled and was pleased with His creations, of which I am one.

A BAD SCRIPT TURNED WORSE

Goetterdaemmerung (Twilight of the Gods)

"If you win, you need not explain.
If you lose, you should not be there
to explain!"

ADOLF HITLER

BACK to April 1945. Just as Mother and I found a three-room cottage with its walls dry and free of mould, the snowdrops and daffodils pushed their heads out of the ground, signifying a new beginning. Our story, which by then already read like a bad script, turned from bad to worse. The Russians with their insignia of the red star, which for us spelt brutal reprisals, pushed their way in from Hungary – the last defensive stand between the German and Russian front. Cannons boomed their dooms-day thunder at all hours of the days and nights. With us trapped in the line of fire.

A new weapon called Stalinorgel (Stalin's organ) a multi-barrelled missile, Katyusha in Russian, wailed its ongoing demoralizing sounds. The mere pressure of the blasts shattered our windows. Our own soldiers were defecting while officers were seen pointing their pistols at them. Stukas (dive bombers) screeched their high-pitched sounds as they dived to empty their bullets. Rumours of a clandestine bunker circulated, where no light dared to penetrate. There apparently were Hitler and Eva and a number of devoted followers who once believed their destiny was to ride through the gates of Valhalla accompanied by the Walkueren hailing their victory. Here Eva's desire to be joined in marriage to her Fuehrer was now fulfilled and the shadow of death closed their eyes. While I imagined Wagner's background notes fading into the distance. Mother and I joined a group heading westward and somehow managed to squeeze into what must have been the last train running, in order to evade the "red invasion," and where the English were rumoured to move in. Then our train was hit and the survivors scrambled to trudge on, imprinting further footprints on the highways of war. We itched from the lice we had inherited from sleeping on the decaying straw spread across the floors of schools that had served the multitude of soldiers and various other fear-infested unwashed bodies.

Collapses can lead to new beginnings and neighbours work together. But instead I observed that as soon as one system deflated and there was a glimpse of hope, the little franchises that had fed on the last regime panicked, not knowing what to do other than to latch on to feed on the next.

These experiences determined in me a conviction that at no time must I allow myself to succumb to any system that wields dominion over another. I dreamed of unity instead, in the hope that the numbers of the willing are rising and, once united, on that day I will cry tears of joy so deep they will collect as a pool around my feet. And that will be the greatest story ever to unfold.

Then just as we settled in another village called Wetzlsdorf, the Russians replaced the English occupation. The Russians were very angry and looked for schnapps to calm their own battle-scarred wounds while the young women went into hiding.

Jonathan

I am sitting at a table outside Starbucks. The two guys sitting at the table next to mine are eyeing the panhandler across the street. "Shouldn't be allowed," one of them says.

"There is a final solution, if you know what I mean," the other acknowledges with a wink. In response, they pound the table and howl with laughter. The traffic is speeding up, half of my coffee spills over the table, the two fix their eyes on me. My head is buzzing. What if I placed an ad requesting a new head – my final solution?

Or to swap my head for another, to experience what it's like to be in someone else's head? It seems to me that if the entire population got into the habit of swapping heads, life would be less complex for the simple reason that we couldn't pretend or excuse our stories by pleading ignorance any longer. Perhaps this is another version of reincarnation and once all aspects are recognized and understood, and the cycle of lessons is complete, you don't have to do this any longer.

Leni

PORTRAITS OF AN INNER LANDSCAPE

(In search of myself)

*"Without an understanding of who we
are and where we come from, I do not
think we can truly advance."*

LOUIS B. LEAKY

I occasionally drop into the church that I pass on my way home from work to immerse myself in its stillness. It is usually at the time of day when the traffic slows, the offices have locked their doors and the shops are shutting down.

The sun projects its fading rays through the stained-glass windows as I settle in one of the benches. Thoughts intrude into the stillness, tumbling over one another, churning up various reflections. According to the medical profession, Jonathan's condition continues to be perceived as a matter of chemicals, and this is repeated like a mantra. A while back it was considered a split in personality, or demonic possession. Are demons capable of invading a mind/body by adjusting their own dose of chemicals to suit their environment?

I get up to light a candle and watch it flicker to life, then I return back to the bench, reflecting on how for years I have tried to make sense of these mental bits and pieces trapped in my head. That ceaselessly rotate preoccupied with the mysteries of fate versus free will, God or no God. Do the glories of heaven exist, the torments of hell? Or the concepts of karma set the stage to enforce the lessons unlearned?

Part of my lessons is to heed the voice that complains: "There is something wrong here," and it's up to me to sort out its concerns. In the long run, I might come to realize that nothing is wrong. Life simply continues to rotate according to its cycles.

Mistakes are when I cling to their concepts; victory is when I learn from them.

On the other hand, were I convinced that Jonathan's condition is a matter of unnegotiable fate, or karma written in stone, I could absolve myself and lay my guilt to rest.

Why does it have to be so complicated?

Or do I make it so?

All right, let's turn the switch off to power down these mental turbines. Either there is nothing other than the dust to dust or ashes to ashes concept, or there is something else, as yet unexamined?

An elderly nun enters from the side door, wearing the headdress of the old habit. She genuflects in front of the altar, lights a candle at the feet of Mary's statue then briskly walks down the aisle. We nod to each other. Does she carry some secret regrets stashed in her vault? If so, what might they be?

When life has gone "wrong," can it be made "right" again? Can I drag the past forward to be jacked up like an old car to be inspected? Or is it that life never goes "wrong," but merely my perception of it does? Life proceeds in cycles of breakdowns and renewals, engaging each cell in its participation, giving me the chance to reinvent myself through myriads of mini reincarnations crammed into this short earthly span. I could polish the tarnished components and refine my personality but they would still be the same components.

It's quiet and peaceful in here devoid of the spoken word, where I can uninterruptedly absorb the silence. My thoughts switch back to Pau, who is now in the beyond. Opposites attract but are not necessarily compatible. "There is nothing a physical workout can't resolve," Pau would say.

While I agreed, I also recognized the importance of the inner world that calls out to be acknowledged, demanding its own law of maintenance. After all, man is not made of flesh alone. When I tried to draw him into my world, he seemed threatened by what he referred as this "self-reflection stuff."

"If you need drama, you can go to the theatre," he would say.

"And where is the partnership?" I would call out.

On the other hand, I know he tried his best. And perhaps I also tried my best. It's just that in each other's eyes and according to our needs and expectations, it wasn't the best after all.

Analysing or succumbing to having the analysis done for me could earn its share of credentials that I could flash like a badge and swap with others. So... could an option of running from guru to guru collecting meditation techniques. But ultimately, I am my own human study, not much different from the others, even if I perceive it to be. Much work is to be done and a fair amount of patience is required to complete the lessons. The sooner I get it over with, the better.

Then I catch myself and say, "What an idiotic statement!" Getting it over with is merely going through the motions of life and it will lose its lustre when I moan and groan and see it as an overload, keeping me hostage to its demands. Such a callous attitude is an insult to my Creator who so lovingly gave me access to these various opportunities, which are the catalyst to my transcendence.

At times, I forget there is a "me," but I appear as a fictitious being. The lesson finally reaches completion the moment I look over my shoulder, anxiously calling, "Where are you?" Then I realize that I am standing close by and have always been unfailingly present. It all begins and ends with me.

At the same time, I must remind myself that there are also spaces in between and that what I project from my mental screen affects everyone else around me. Therefore, my first commandment must be to be good to myself so that I can be good to others. This at times proves to be a great challenge. After all, I am the queen of suffering, and being good to myself is a challenge. And the prospect of retirement without a schedule in place, the thought of being left to watch the script of my own movie, is a concern. I might not like what I see and my investments might not match up to my expectations. On the other hand, who is my primary investment, if not myself? I succumb to my previous advice: "Go home and cultivate a good relationship with yourself." Connected, I am strong and I can remove my armour. Once I get to know myself, I can un-judgmentally invite others into my world.

According to the bible scriptures, Jesus spent forty days and nights in the wilderness tapping into the tribulations of being human. Buddha sat forty-nine days and nights under the Bodhi tree and apparently didn't move "until he got it." The Egyptian initiates shut themselves inside a sarcophagus of sensory deprivation to face their daemons.

The Essene Gospel of Peace has this to say: "In the moment of breathing in and breathing out are hidden all the mysteries." Perhaps all I have to do is to breathe in and breathe out. On the other hand, I don't even have to do that – my body does it for me when I don't interfere.

Admittedly, a present-day vision quest appears more difficult amidst today's noisy city sprawl and hectic schedule surrounded by towering buildings and covered by stretches of concrete preventing contact with the soil.

Beware of succumbing to the temptations of the material daemon's focused on self-interest, I tell myself. Should they show up, it's up to me how to deal with them and one must expect a great deal of resistance.

LESSONS

"The seed falling among the thorns
refers to someone who hears the word,
but the worries of this life and
the deceitfulness of wealth choke
the word, making it
unfruitful."

MATTHEW 13:22

STRIVING is always looking, but misses out on the seeing.

This I read somewhere.

One of my teachers is called reaction. When I step back, I can observe myself in action. The observer is observing the observer – another movie reeling by. In this script, I show up as this creature anxiously trying to trick time by racing ahead in securing a carefree material future environment for Jonathan and me to settle in. This requires a great deal of planning with little time to slack off and enjoy a picnic in the present.

I actually did well in this department and congratulated myself on my good judgment that showed a good return on my investments. Until I woke up one morning and to my horror discovered, that I found my investments had plummeted to what seemed an irretrievable level, and faith in myself caved in. I discovered a side of myself I wasn't proud of as the various personalities I had culti-vated showed up. The most challenging to deal with, was the victim personality who failed to understand why after "trying so hard," fate had withheld its expected rewards, and I asked heaven to intervene. But heaven remained too far away, with the communication line seemingly overloaded by other needy souls with similar requests.

The display of self-blame and endless criticism that followed was unbearable, to a point where I couldn't stand to be around myself any longer. I had no spot to drop anchor, trapped in a dreary world assessed in terms of material gains and losses. Compassion was nowhere to be found. I felt I had forsaken both Jonathan and myself. Instead, of pausing to give myself a break, I compulsively pushed forward with a drive to recapture the losses. And it takes great courage to rechart the routine with its established programming tenaciously holding on to its unyielding interpretations. While I longed to run through the forest dancing with the trees and surrender to the embrace of a lover.

Play with my angels, where the past becomes united with the present and the anticipated future has no limits. A world in which the impossible becomes possible and we release our passion and become lovers of our lives.

Where my friends and I cross the boundaries, we declared couldn't be done – the cluttered corners can be uncluttered, the magic of childhood reclaimed.

Life no longer needs to be edited and we can step out of the script, even glow in the dark and live in our own nonsense. The magic will be in the sharing. Infusing each other with energy.

"Anyone who has never made a mistake
has never tried anything new."

ALBERT EINSTEIN

After a period of self-torture and continuing to implore divine help that still seemed slow in coming, I knew the source of my suffering could only be found in my memory bank stuck in the past.

Having taken note of the increasing numbers of homeless inhabiting the downtown streets, I vowed that Jonathan would always be financially provided for. After all, my own mother hadn't lived to a ripe old age and Jonathan's estate had to show a good return. At the same time and after further investigation a bitter resentment welled up at life's betrayal for having imposed on me the father's role as sole provider after Pau could no longer hold down a job. A father's role in my book had to be strong, make money and be a good provider, and I dutifully followed this rule. But now I questioned whether the result of trying to keep pace with this masculine-driven side as I perceived it, contrary to my personality, had resulted in disconnectedness and burnout, and I had lost touch with my feminine essence. My query flared up an email correspondence among my friends.

The first reply to my quandary was:

> "That makes sense to me, Leni. On
> the other hand, maybe these times
> of burnout are necessities to allow

chaos to shake things up to examine its components?" Love and light, Pat

Yes, dear Pat, your reply awakened certain aspects that need examining: But at present, my negative state of disconnectedness is certainly not contributing to stability and my brain could clearly use some re-programming. Leni

Ann Moffatt: I don't find it hard to believe that a woman trying to make it in a male establishment is a recipe for burnout. You've done better than most Leni, and you've carried a heavy emotional load on top of that – and I don't think you've lost your feminine essence. I'm not sure what more this deep unhappiness you're feeling now can teach you. You are already wise in so many ways. I love Pat's idea of burnout being a necessity that allows chaos to shake things up. I've found so often in life that burning out on one thing opens the door to something else. Love, Ann

Gennie: Such wisdom from y'all ... I agree with Ann that Leni you definitely don't seem to me to have lost your feminine essence and I see you as creative, elegant and wise, and you're not the only one whose brain needs re-programming – mine does too & I too believe it can be done – how fortunate for us to be exposed to ways of doing so! Love, Gennie

My reply: Each one of you is right, dear wise sisters. Your precious encouragement is appreciated. The personalities that arise cannot be easily dismissed, however, but are calling to be dealt with. As my friend Eva said, they need to evolve and wake up to hopefully learn sooner rather than later what they needed from that particular experience. I am touched by your support
Love and Light to all of us. Leni

This correspondence evoked a past vision:

In that vision, I am sitting in the company of my cosmic counsellors prior to my present reincarnation. Family, country, gender and the date of birth are carefully considered for my evolutionary advancement with a checklist placed in front of me.

After lengthy contemplation, I pick up the list and begin ticking off my choice of experiences to be completed this time around, then push the list their way.

Having consulted the list, they look at each other then turn to face me with what I perceive to be concern in their eyes.

"Hasty," one says.

"An overload," remarks another.

It seems that the number of choices are evidently a concern. The overload could result in burnout, which might have to be impressed in an even harsher way some other time around by perpetuating the search.

Undeterred, I adamantly declare I want to experience the entire spectrum of the human journey this time around. Then I point out that according to the cosmic law, the final choice is mine, even at the prospect of messing it up. The contract is signed and sealed with the customary double spiral.

"If we are not happy and joyous at this
season,
for what other season shall we wait
and for what other time shall we look?
This is a day of joy,
a time of happiness,
a period of spiritual growth."

ABDUL-BAHA,
Awakening to the Ultimate Reality

KATHARINA NOLLA

THE BOOK OF LIFE

"Until you make the unconscious
conscious, it will direct your life and you
will call it fate."

CARL JUNG

PERHAPS my higher soul-self in its wisdom will sabotage my success where further lessons are still necessary instead of trying to skip my apprenticeship in graduating to mastery.

There is so much I want to know that perhaps I will only come to know when I no longer am compelled to know. I have always known that when I grow up, I will write my book. Have I finally grown up?

Growing up, means maturity. It means doing my homework, in charge of myself, being fully accountable for my actions and reactions.

It requires patience, the responsibility to rest and nurture myself from preventing becoming a liability to others.

After weeks of self-torture still ruminating about the financial losses I incurred, judging myself harshly, I asked, "Am I dying?"

Self-torture is not exactly a virtue, is the answer, and who says that I must always know better? It is I of course, who says I must, and the truth dawns on me that in the background the child at the turn of events had come to perceive poverty as a form of punishment and as a mother I vowed that my child and I would never be poor, as I once was.

At the same time, I remind myself that the universe doesn't recognize mistakes but merely different states of being: cycles of composting, breakdowns and renewal. I am part of this cycle and there is yet another side to the story still in the making.

SELF-FULFILLING PROPHECIES

EACH town and village in our region celebrated its annual festivity called Kirchweih. It was a consecration honouring the patron saint of its particular community. On that day, the circus came to town; the gypsies set up their tables complete with their crystal balls and fanned out cards to predict the future. The Ferris wheel was assembled and vendors hawked their trinkets. Family and friends gathered to feast on entire roasted piglets, consumed in one sitting, while the smell of compôte, pastries and other delicacies permeated the house. On that day Father, Mother and I set off to visit my "other Oma," as I called her – father's mother, to celebrate this holiday, although she didn't reciprocate the visits on account of grandfather, whom she didn't approve of. Their patron saint was St. Sebastian. This Oma was tall with pale skin that stretched tightly over her cheekbones in a way that reminded me of the Roman sculptures I had seen in a history book. This paternal Oma would scrutinize me like the priest during confession, while she questioned mother about my cooking and sewing progress. When it became clear that I failed to measure up to her standards, she asked, "What *can* she do?"

"She can write poetry and paint pictures of flowers," Mother answered in a faltering voice. By then I was already aware that in the society I was born into, such skills were not of high priority in the running of a household and in becoming a good wife to look after her husband's household and his children.

She would hand me the traditional Lebkuchen doll, decorated with blue eyes and rosy-red cheeks that was the customary gift for children on that day. It was also customary to give money to buy trinkets off the stalls and to spend on the Ferris wheel.

On one occasion, I lost the money she had given me, and it was pointed out that I had been careless on a previous occasion, and she said to Father, "You had better find her a good husband who will know how to manage the money."

Father laughed and said, "Yes, managing money is not part of her personality." From then on, the money for trinkets and such was entrusted to Father.

"I will show you that I can," I said, and they laughed again.

At times life seems to deliver its self-fulfilling prophecies, while fate is the collaborator in writing the script, to be translated.

WAR CHILD –
A PARTY INTERRUPTED

NOVEMBER 25 1944: I am standing on a chair by the window with my new dress draped across the back of the chair. Ribbons are tied in my hair. The smell of freshly baked cakes and cookies drifts through the house in preparation for celebrating my name day. While I scan the courtyard, I draw flowers on the misty pane. Then I wipe it clean, waiting for the sight of my Tati to appear, then cloud it over with my breath and this time, draw a fire-breathing dragon.

The following memory replays itself like a black and white movie. The figure of an exhausted man walks into the courtyard. A young woman with the features of a Dresden doll runs out of the door. The little girl jumps off the chair and she too dashes out of the door. The three fall into each other's arms, crying and laughing. Tati has arrived just in time, as I dreamed he would.

"Is the war over?" I ask.

My parents look into each other's eyes and stop laughing. But Tati is back and even Otati – prone to argumentative moods, appeared glad to see him.

Tati is considering a drive out to Berak but Otati doesn't think it's a good idea. I am excited, I want to come too, but they say, no, I can't.

Later, I am woken by their voices and hear they were shot at by the Partisans, who they said were taking control of the countryside and that several estates and factories had been targeted and looting was rampant. New fires were glowing in the night and no one seemed to be in control of putting them out and tomorrow night it could be our turn to go up in flames.

THE SECRET I HAVE BEEN CARRYING THROUGHOUT THE YEARS

THE door opened. It was I who turned the knob, slowly, before closing it again.

In the semi-darkness of the room, slumped in his chair with muffled sobs escaping his chest sat my Tati. "All is lost, Berak is gone," he announced to the room. Later, he appeared with two suitcases filled with money notes. "You might need it," he said to mother.

I was ten years old. From there on, the material world always proved a challenge that I could never quite trust, it became my ongoing nemesis that I had to test over and over throughout the years. I envisioned that one day, to have the means – in honour of his memory to retrieve the magic of his beloved Berak back.

In the morning, still in my nightie, I ran out looking for him but he had gone.

"He didn't want to wake you," Oma said. Mother was crying. "He took great risks in coming to see us," Oma added.

From there on, nothing made sense. It was the last time I saw him alive. His body was found in a field, marked with signs of torture and flies buzzing around.

THE CONSEQUENCES OF THE COLLECTIVE EGO

*"You've got to forget about this civilian. Whenever
you drop bombs, you're going to hit civilians."*

BERRY GOLDWATER

WHEN Mother and I arrived in Austria, the cityscapes appeared like a dismal black and white movie, with grey figures flitting through the bombed-out streets, scrounging through the rubble. Bedraggled columns of displaced women and children, like Mother and me, clogged the highways, babies were strapped onto their mother's back, with toddlers clinging to their skirts; the aged required assistance. But this was not a movie with actors playing a part. These were real people – us.

Others arrived by horse-drawn wagons or travelled by car often abandoned by the side of the road for lack of fuel, or blown-out tires. The two suitcases of money notes had long ago landed in someone else's hands, and the little left over became valueless currency that the Tito regime converted from the kuna to the dinar. With winter settling in, a piece of firewood was considered a treasure, as was a handful of coal. Stories of missing sons, fathers and husbands pining away in prison camps were on everyone's lips. In this new country, we were again a minority, this time a minority living in squalor, considered a liability in this already overcrowded land. Along the way I would anxiously scan each train station we passed, asking if they might have seen my Oma, who had to be left behind and might have been sent by train. "Her name is Theresia Possert," I said.

"When will we see her again?" I asked Mother. But my questions merely produced an uncontrollable flow of tears. And in the back of everyone's mind was still the hope that by some miracle the borders would open ... we would return and everything would be as it once was.

"Draw the curtain, Leni, the light is too harsh, my head is splitting." It's Mother's voice – just her and me now, sharing the small room streaked with mould belonging to an old farmhouse in Eastern Styria on the way to Hungary. Sometimes for days she won't leave the room. It's like living in a morgue.

"Make me some chamomile tea, Leni."

"Oh, this soup is tasteless, what did you put in it?"

Of course, the weak flavour of the soup is a matter of scarcity and what I did not put into it. I try my best to create some sense of cheerfulness in this dingy room we live in. I collect twigs of graceful shapes pointing through the snow and arrange them in a pretty bottle I found.

I scrub the mold from the walls and the window, at Christmas I weave branches of holly along its sill. No Christmas tree nor festive candles graced our room and Christmas dinner consisted of half a dozen shriveled potatoes salted with mother's tears.

My clothes are not adjusting to my height. One of my shoes has a hole in it, but I fuss with her hair and mine. And I desperately need some order in my life.

A fast-forward to my home in Victoria

"Look at me. What a pathetic heap I have become," I said to myself, back in the present, still immersed in ruminating over my financial loss. I knew more suffering would be in store if I didn't sort this out. As I'd told Ida, if I treated others as I at times treat myself, I'd be charged for criminal assault.

I had lost my will to eat. The mere thought of stepping near the stove evoked a feeling of nausea. It seemed clear that bouts of depression are negative attitudes directed at myself. In a state of depression, I manufacture chemicals that don't serve me. What does this kind of viewpoint say about myself? My viewpoints spin my stories, which in turn weave the destiny of my life. THIS ME – THE I AM THAT I AM.

Yet even after I gradually pulled myself into daylight again, the losses continued to show up on a cloudy day with the ego already trying to gain renewed control. While the old insecurity licked its tongue in anticipation of more food to feed on.

Invite them in. They are your other half knocking, I told myself. Allow them to explain their concerns, and listen. I instinctively knew that the issue of money wasn't merely about money. It is a convoluted bargaining system about self-esteem and identity. A collection of stories that sort the world into gain and loss, preventing me from partaking of the food paradise has to offer. I am my own human lesson, wrapped in a package unique only to me, which no other school could have taught.

I must once again remind myself that yesterday is already gone and tomorrow is yet an elusive shadow, but that I always have access to the present from which to move forward and that apathy spells spiritual suicide.

Meanings: Regardless of the meanings I attach to my reactions, they remain but meanings. Only once I associate them with their source, can I liberate myself from their dependence.

Jonathan

I am sitting on top of a cliff overlooking the ocean. Gulls circle above. They have discovered an air current so they glide with motionless wings, taking advantage of the free ride. I am wondering what has led to the demise of Atlantis? "And are we heading in a similar direction?" I ask my Maker.

MESSAGE FROM THE MEMORY OF ATLANTIS

They said of him to whom the overseeing of the continent was entrusted, "He shines like a star." His was a long and glorious history. He was called The One.

The motto of Atlantis was "Do no harm to your Self so as to prevent harm to others."

The second motto was the ageless "To thine own Self be true."

The people of Atlantis lived in houses supported by elegant arches. Excess was not a way of life. Each garment was stitched and woven with utmost care and of great beauty; the materials were recycled so that nothing was wasted. Investments, profits and land speculations – as in our present, played no role in their interaction. Equal wages were paid to all, no more no less, even to The One who shone like a star.

After The One had fulfilled his role on his continent and departed for his other journey, the populace gathered in honour of his soul, as was customary throughout the history of Atlantis.

The celebration consisted of a second stage – the selection of a new overseer to be welcomed and initiated into his or her all-important role.

At this time, a brilliant scientist lived in the land who possessed what they called great mind power. His name was Hoira. At the height of the ceremony in honour of the departed, Hoira surprisingly projected his own image to flash in the sky. "I have an announcement to make," he proclaimed through his image.

The population reacted in stunned silence, a sea of faces stared up in disbelief, for what occurred was an unprecedented interruption of the ritual in honour of The One.

"This time no election is to take place," Hoira announced, then smiled and said, "The elected is present."

With that, he extended his hand and one long gasp rose from the crowd. What presented itself before their eyes was clearly a product of science, for beside Hoira stood in the radiance of his youth, a replica of The One. It was an act contrary to the law of nature and clearly out of character with the legacy of The One.

Shattering the silence, one united cry rose into the air. It sounded like an explosion racing through the land, terrible and awesome. "No-o-o-o!"

Undeterred, Hoira's image continued to hover in the sky with a triumphant smile playing on his lips. While the population huddled in groups and their words, previously a melodious flow now tripped and tumbled over each other. They went home and said no more but returned the following day to insist on their right to an election. At the same time they understood that to reclaim the harmony of the land, they had to unite in deep meditation, centring with the all-prevailing cosmic soul and with each other. In their hearts, they understood that the young man, a replica of The One now standing at Hoira's side, was not to be judged. Bound by their love for all beings and each other, he must be embraced as their own but they must not be deprived of their right to an election.

Hoira, however, would not yield to their request and from then on the land experienced rumblings of interference from behind the increasingly fortified walls of the building. The building that had once been accessible to all now Hoira, with the youth as his guest, were 'chauffeured' through the streets, an act unheard of in the memory of the generations. It was clear from the clothes he and his companion wore that the old dress code of three garments applied no more, but now appeared in many designs to flatter the beauty of the youth.

Groups of young people began to hang around the building. They became known as the Runalongers because they ran alongside the limousine, calling the youth's name, copying his style – a trend that gradually created a rift between the old code and the new. Strange words were added to the vocabulary – property, position and privilege. "What do they mean?" the population asked as they gathered in the streets. The Runalongers self-chosen translators of the new law laughed and acted in a superior way, and a fog of secrecy settled over the land.

KATHARINA NOLLA

Leni

FOOTPRINTS ALONG THE HIGHWAY OF LIFE

"Some self-exploration in the moment might not be a bad investment."

KATHARINA NOLLA

Journaled from Leni's home in Victoria

IT'S up to me how I respond to life's challenges, and what footprints I imprint along the highway of my life. Or what boundaries I set. The lessons don't have to show up on a dramatic or heroic scale to earn recognition, but might gain importance from any daily interaction. Even if I am just a tiny cog in the wheel of life. In the overall design, I am not too small to make a difference.

"You have to come over to do something about the spiders," my new tenant demanded one night at two a.m. during my novice landlord days. "They are huge!" I crawled out of bed and drove over.

I found indeed such an invasion – of three spiders, and they looked like ordinary spiders to me.

A couple of weeks later, there was an issue with her neighbour apparently peeking in her window. Then it went back to the nocturnal spiders again.

"They are huge," she repeated. "I can show them to you, I trapped them in a jar." By then, my patience was wearing thin and I said to myself:

Now let's look at this situation closely and ask what can be learned from it, I told myself.

Boundaries: I clearly needed a set of boundaries. "How about going outside to release them from their imprisonment," I suggested.

"I am not going outside at this time of night."

"I can understand," I said, shedding my victim role. "I likewise don't want to go outside at this time of night."

At that moment, I determined that how she acts is her business, but how I react is mine.

What if I had a choice to relocate to an environment where the answers were clearly spelled out and served in neat little packages, instead of running around doing the guessing game and dying with myriads of unanswered questions still on my lips?

It's evident that according to my personality, I would decline this approach but prefer the role of the explorer, a home-grown product that in the end I could take pride in.

I step back and take further inventory of this so-called financial devastation as I perceive it.

On the other hand, a win-win situation can only be sustained by someone else's losses and is not known for being a faithful companion. It becomes evident that nothing is as it used to be in this rapidly changing time, where the Earth is trembling under my feet, the wells drying up and the established formulas failing to apply any longer; while some long for the good old days.

At this point in time I question whether restoration of the old system is really the answer and whether we should spend time and energy relying on a model where everyone is running around doing a patch-up job, trying to patch what in the first place had never been fully predictable. In the mean-time we might run out of tape while yearning for the simplicity of a refined beginning that is beckoning on the horizon. I certainly wouldn't want to miss this opportunity or the ecstasy that is waiting on the other side.

Next four pages from Jonathan's Trunk in the basement

After my shower this morning reflecting in the steamed-up mirror, I saw a zipper stitched to the skin of my chest, partly zipped down, exposing the rawness of my chest. I tried to zip it up but it was jammed.

I am inside this body assigned to me but at times the true me occupying this body escapes and I become an empty vessel. Something is missing, but I don't know what it is.

I am back sitting on the familiar patio of the psych ward. I invite the sun to kiss my cheek but at the sight of me, it goes into hiding. At the other end of the patio a girl is tearing sheets of papers from a book, screaming, "He plagiarized my memories he immortalized in his book!"

Two guys are seated at the table next to mine. One of them is wearing a hat while the other has a seagull feather stuck in his hair. The one with the feather is pointing to the flowers in a bottle that someone must have left behind. "Interrupting their seeding process is a crime against nature," he says.

The other contemplates this before saying, "I was a twin once."

"Then what happened?"

"The other half died."

Their eyes gaze into space as if waiting for a revelation. The one wearing the hat begins to fidget, saying that he is dying for a smoke.

They leave.

A bird hops onto the table, taking the opportunity to peck at the crumbs left behind. It cocks its head as a shadow spreads across the table, outlining the silhouette of a female body. The bird resumes its pecking. The shadow body is about to lower itself into the vacant chair, then hesitates and points to the one next to mine, and I understand that this is out of consideration for disturbing the bird.

"My name is Itak," she says.

"What kind of name is that," I wonder.

She reaches for the magazine left on the table and spells the name for me. The way she pronounces it, it sounds like Eetahk, with a drawn-out ee. It's hard to determine her exact age, but she's young and pleasant to look at.

"It is an Idrisian name," she answers.

"Where is Idris?"

This time, she pulls a napkin from her pocket, then draws a map and spells out the name.

I look at the scribbles, but can't make sense of them, nor of the map.

It is their indigenous name, she tells me. "Translated into your language, it means Butterfly System," then she excuses herself and leaves.

ITAK'S EXPEDITION

"WHAT compelled you to land on our planet?" I asked, when next we met.

"It wasn't a plan – it was by accident."

This was her story:

The crew's assignment was to measure the evolutionary vibrations of certain planets. Ours was not on their list, she said, and they were not to land unless so specified. When they set out on their assignment over Planet J, Hira their pilot muttered something about the advantage of direct contact versus instruments. This meant he was in favour of a landing.

Most of the crew protested against his decision because it was contrary to their plan. Hira argued that within a short period, they could teach this backward population on Planet J to improve their farming skills and their transportation system, and no one would miss the extra time spent on a good cause.

An argument ensued, the majority of the crew seemed tempted by the proposal. A vote was suggested, ignoring the warning that such interplanetary interaction could regress the evolutionary process.

When they landed, the inhabitants bowed and chanted Yooyoo, yooyoo, which their interpreter Yared, translated as Gods. "The Gods have returned," and they clearly expected gifts. Yared explained to them that they weren't Gods, but simply inhabitants from another planet. They responded by pointing to the sky, the airship as they called it had come from the sky and that is where they believed the Gods lived.

A multitude gathered in front of a building that towered over the others. The news circulated that the king would display his gifts from the Gods. The crew looked at each other and when they looked at Hira, he evaded their eyes. A procession of musicians, scantily dressed female dancers bedecked in colourful plumes jumped onto a stage, clearly in celebration of the occasion. Closer and closer, they interacted, while the spectators moaned and some swooned at the sight of the aroused male genitals, while Hira's eyes expressed an unusual gleam.

Next, a hush fell over the scene. Two men stepped forward blowing into long instruments and a flash of light reflected from the stage.

"He has acquired the radiance of the sun," the crowd whispered to each other and the crew realized that this was their king. In surprise, they looked at the cape the king wore that so awed the crowd, and recognized it as the piece of material that their crew-mate Esor had looped together from a variety of shiny interplanetary threads she had collected, including an elaborate container made from the same material that served as a crown. Esor had the endearing creativity of a child. Clearly the king admired such shining objects so Hira had persuaded her to present them as a gift. "He has acquired the radiance of the sun," the crowd repeated, while the king smiled proudly.

According to Hira's expression, it was clear that his focus was beyond the interest of agriculture and the transportation system, but in the interaction between the sexes. Such outer-planetary interactions were condoned only when they were part of a higher plan and compatible with the advancement of the race. The crew became concerned. They had seen the unfortunate consequences of such unions. They were mutants who lived in abhorrent isolation, for the inhabitants treated them cruelly. They called them "The Curse."

Hira however, argued that occasionally the offspring of such a union would inherit the seed of superior stature, which they call the sons of Gods.

I was told that after the experience on Planet J, Hira clearly no longer seemed in control of their craft, and in the vicinity of Planet H – our planet – they trailed off course and had to resort to an emergency landing.

"Why the alphabetical order of the names?" I asked and she explained that according to the planets' evolutionary scale from one to ten, in alphabetical order ours would rate as H – eight, that is – as hers once was during its more primitive stage.

"So, ours is merely two points below the lowest?"

She nodded.

"On what scale is yours now?"

"C – three, that is. There are more highly evolved scales, of course, but these are still inaccessible to us."

"What happened to your ship? Surely, if you are telling the truth, it would have been discovered by our authorities by now, or the media-hounds would have sniffed it out."

The two guys from the previous day showed up with their cigarettes stuck in their mouth puffing like two chimneys, while the two security guards pointed to the "No smoking" sign, and ordered everyone to clear the patio and return to our rehabilitation paradise.

Leni

THE MOST VALUABLE LESSON IS IN THE HEALING

A few days ago, Ida told me about a Hawaiian healing method called ho-opono-pono, and that through this method an entire hospital of mentally ill patients was cured. I asked her how it works.

"Come to the workshop next week," she suggested.

When we arrived, we found that the workshop had been cancelled.

Later, I met someone who had taken the workshop previously and I asked her if this method also applied on the ancestral level. She confirmed that it did. Her confirmation recalled the time when I saw Otati bolt from his sleep with his fingers wrapped around an imaginary trigger. Or he would break out in a sweat and Oma said it was the malaria he caught in the trenches while fighting in Salonika during the first Balkan War. Another time I overheard her say there must be a curse on this family and Ivanka, who seemed versed on this subject, explained that a curse is something that settles on your shoulders and wraps itself around your neck. Its grip can never be broken unless you find the right magic. Maybe a bit of ho-opono-pono could have made a difference then.

The times Tati was absent, I was assigned to sleep in grandmother's bed, in the room that she and grandfather shared. At times grandfather's voice boomed like a crash of thunder directed at Oma, alluding to some kind of betrayal, and she would defend herself by saying, "I didn't know their intent, they said they were old friends from way back during the time in Solonika, that's why I let them in."

It was as though demons had settled in that room that stoked the dissension, feeding on its sustenance, of which they apparently couldn't get enough. During such times, I would dash to Mother's room, shivering under my nightie drenched with cold perspiration while Ivanka's words echoed back about the curse. Instead, I found Mother with her head burrowed under her pillows while obscure shapes flickered on the walls and ceilings, dancing in a contorted choreography. A stench of scorched hair and burned flesh hung in the air. "The devil is here!" I screamed, while the house went numb with a fear so powerful that no tool could smash. I recognized that there was another war raging here.

Is this what the Old Testament meant when it referred to wrestling with the angel of darkness? Maybe a bit of Ho-opono-pono could have done the trick. At that moment, an additional vow was added on my list: I will not exit this planet without having resolved my own struggle with the forces of darkness I inherited in this room. Witnessing the pain inflicted on each other by the people I loved, I recognized that the most valuable lesson is in the healing that can break the curse, and that I will take on the role of the saviour who will transform this household to a state of bliss filled with light. I will become the catalyst that breaks this ancestral spell.

But in the end, it seemed I failed. One by one, they died without the bliss I had anticipated to see on their faces. What kind of saviour could I be? So I shut away my dreaming. And I wondered if my grandparents recognized the harm they inflicted on that child trapped in their room.

Translated, Ho-opono-pono means, "I am sorry, please forgive me, thank you, I love you." The man sitting next to me sharing the workshop wanted to know if someone is a jerk and rages accusations at me, why should he say I love and forgives him?

Good question, I thought, then concluded that to me, it means, "I am sorry things aren't going for you as you would like them to, and that could be another catalyst, and merely listening could do the trick."

MY NEURONS
FIRING THE FUEL

"Forgiveness is not always easy.
At times, it feels more painful than the
wound re suffered, to forgive the one that
inflicted it. And yet, there is no peace
without forgiveness."

MARIANNE WILLIAMS

MANY years later, after I became a mother myself, and little Jonathan would come running to our bed, Pau ordered him back to his room

While I protested against Pau's orders, he insisted that the little guy must learn to be strong. Arguments would erupt between us and in the end I shrank from my husband's voice, echoing beside me like a clash of thunder, while the chips of my brain scanned for an association. With my neurons firing up the fuel to spark a connection, like my own mother, I shut down and froze in my emotional tracks.

It is a memory that has returned to haunt me, harsh and unforgiving, stalking through the nights, eliciting a confession. Didn't I know what I was doing to my child in that room, by bailing out? What kind of saviour is this? And so, the stage was set to pace with my guilt cradled in my arms.

KATHARINA NOLLA

At the same time, I imagined what it must have been for mother trapped in the hostile environment between these two people who were her parents and must have asked the same question, once: "...Didn't they know what they were doing to that child in that room next to theirs?"

"Here you go again," my friend Chuck would say when Jonathan thrashed through another episode. "Running around trying to save Jonathan, you are not living your life role; you are living Jonathan's." Arguments would erupt between us that eventually damaged our relationship.

"The intuitive mind is a sacred gift and the rational mind is a faithful servant. We have created a society that honours the servant and has forgotten the gift."

ALBERT EINSTEIN

One night, as I tossed and turned with the accusations of my guilt cranked up, I realized that being immersed in such emotions means I am not rationally present, either for myself or Jonathan nor Chuck. It's a vast desolation with no oasis in sight. It seemed to me that no one should be issued a licence for motherhood with such unresolved emotions clinging to her psyche. And I once more renewed my childhood vow of not exiting this planet before having resolved my struggle with the forces of darkness. At the same time, I must give credit to the little Leni whose vigilance had written the script kept on hold for me the adult

Leni, to ultimately discover, and to liberate myself from the imprisonment of my hereditary past. Therefore, I believe that each of us has access to the guidelines of our own ultimate salvation. One merely has to look for the source and trust in the wisdom of the messages that show up. Digging through the past then is not a waste of time after all. I never thought about thanking the little Leni for her gift of courage to have hung in there.

Then she simply disappeared one day. "What happened to you?" I ask now that I have re-connected with her in the present.

"You should know what happened. Due to the circumstances, I chose a fast-forward to grow up, having decided that being vulnerable no longer seemed to resolve anything other than contribute to sadness."

Again I thank my Creator for the capacity of my storage room – and for keeping my memories on hold until such time as I am ready to sort through and deal with them. Admittedly at times it gets pretty crowded in there.

Can I become my own saviour? I can at least give it a try. I recall Fear's advice: "Cross the bridge often and learn the lesson of compassion."

Do our stories keep the universe entertained? I know there are times when they keep me entertained and maybe one day, I might make mine into a movie. Instead of it being a heavy drama, it might turn out to be a comedy full of nonsense, to make me and my friends burst out laughing.

Or maybe, I don't have to wait. The present pages might already contain enough of that.

A KALEIDOSCOPE OF STORIES

Further Memories

HEAT waves danced like playful ghosts through the lazy afternoon as my newly discovered friend Marica and I sat in the cool arbour of her house. We were six years old. Even though we were related and had known of each other, we hadn't met before now because of the deep dissension between Otati's family and us. Marica's mother was Otati's much younger sister. I once overheard Otati refer to his sister as "that snob," and cursed his father. I knew she was married to a successful Croatian businessman and had two daughters, Nadja and Marica, the younger of the two, and they lived in a beautiful house.

I don't know what prompted Tati to drop me off that day. Maybe he had business connections with the husband and decided to take me along.

The sweet scent of jasmine and honeysuckle drifted through the air while Marica and I were immersed in playing hostesses by pouring imaginary tea into miniature china cups, which we served to Marica's dolls, lined up in a row on a bench. Then suddenly the peaceful afternoon was shattered by a voice crashing through the courtyard, "I am going to kill her!" and the sobbing of a young girl in the background.

Startled by the interruption crashing through the yard, I looked at Marica and wordlessly asked, "Here too?" No verbal communication was necessary as her eyes confirmed, "Yes, here too," while the dolls lined up on the bench looked on with placid eyes and we proceeded to pour the tea. At that moment, I understood that within the genteel demeanour of this house, brewed generations of unchecked emotions wielding their hatchets from a past directed at the present. And before my eyes filed an uninterrupted column of bodies, a vision I couldn't understand then, but it awakened in me a deep feeling of compassion. Then a conciliatory voice was heard, the sounds of doors opening and clanging shut, and I understood that this column of bodies, although not of this world, was related. They were my ancestral lineage passing through.

Jonathan's
Page

I'M trudging through a tunnel strewn with litter I'm supposed to sweep up, but I don't have a broom.

Besides, visibility is poor. I hear a sarcastic snicker and a voice saying, "It's up to you to solve the puzzle."

"What puzzle are you talking about?"

My eyes adjust. I see that one of the walls has human heads mounted on it and I understand this is a dream about my ancestral gallery. What I have to sweep away is the garbage they left behind.

I pick up an unidentifiable object then another and another, flinging them against the wall. "It's you who left this mess behind, and now you expect me to clean it up!" I scream.

Their mummified faces turn and writhe in an attempt to evade the assault. Suddenly, I feel sorry for them. They're stuck, mounted on the wall without even the use of hands to shield themselves.

"All right, where is the fucking broom?" Then I realize they're dead and they don't know they are dead. At the end of the tunnel, near the exit, the outline of a body is visible. It's Mother and she is blocking the door. "Where is the goddamn broom?" I yell at her.

Then I realize she has no broom either. She walks towards me. She's carrying a flashlight, which throws a weak thread of light as it weaves its way, guiding us to snake around the litter, before aiming for the exit. I am sorry to have yelled at her. One day I want to live a counter-story for her. I know she is writing a book, she says it's helping her resolve her memories and I reassured her she could include my pages.

Leni

FURTHER KALEIDOSCOPES

HERE in Victoria I discovered a small restaurant where one can have one's tea leaves read to predict the future. While travelling through the Middle East, I had my coffee grounds read in Cairo. When I came back, I said to myself I will try this, and casually rotated my cup while contemplating the coffee grounds that had arranged themselves into two distinct mosaic images.

The first mosaic showed an image of an Egyptian priestess wearing the headdress of the Goddess Hathor sitting in front of a square black box, while the other side of the box, frantically ejected sheets of papers. The prediction of the box spitting out sheets of paper became clear to me the day I sat in front of my first computer with the printer churning out the pages, predicting my imminent book. But what was the priestess trying to project?

The second mosaic that showed up was a replica of two antiquated cabooses parked at the bottom of a hill as shown to me during my drugged-out state of Jonathan's delivery with an ether mask slapped over my face. Immersed in that ether fog I was then given to understand that my baby's survival and my own depended on me pushing these cabooses up the hill with my baby inside one of them. After the delivery, with my brain still in a woozy state, I asked about the sutures and the doctor confirmed that it had been a difficult delivery. I was unsure what to make of this overall vision and asked that it be revealed one day.

THE SEARCH

ONE day during his mid teens, Jonathan suddenly disappeared, but this time I knew this was not his regular pattern.

After weeks of frantic search and sleepless nights, I received a call from my friend Peg who lived on the West Coast before it became a national park. We used to rent one of Peg's beachfront cottages when Jonathan was a child. At this time the now world-renowned Long Beach area was still a small community after the U. S. draft dodgers invaded the area, squatting on Florencia Bay or Wreck Beach as the locals call it, on account of its shipwrecks. Through the "grapevine" Peg found out that Jonathan was seen "squatting" on an uninhabited island in the Clayoquot Sound area, west of Tofino.

I reserved one of Peg's cottages and packed for the trip via Port Alberni and over the then-unpaved gravel road. My brain seemed a barren wasteland with tumbleweed racing through. As in the past, tears eluded me as I navigated the switchbacks over the mountains, still brooding on my mother guilt.

Eight hours later, when I arrived at the beach, the foghorn was bellowing like a Minotaur, rain pelting on the roofs of the cottages, and storm winds whipping the trees. Stretched out in front of the stove I could see tongues of flame and Peg's cats sitting in the glow, obsessed with their eternal task of grooming. If only life could remain like this, basking in domestic simplicity. But I knew a challenging task lay ahead.

After several inquiries, a local fisherman named Jack agreed to take me to the island where Jonathan was reportedly "squatting" and once the storm had subsided, we boarded his boat.

The surface of the ocean now appeared smooth and satiny. The shore, left behind, became a background of anchored fishing boats blending into the landscape, while the houses gazed placidly out to sea.

Cormorants flew silently in pairs, with an occasional solitary straggler, all in one direction. The boat, ploughing steadily through the water, created illusionary crystal Pegasus wings on either side of the bow. Uninhabited mini islands gave the appearance of fortresses erupted from the ocean. We passed Cat Face Mountain shaved bare by logging except for a cluster of scrawny trees giving the mountain the appearance of a scraggly beard.

After an hour, Jack pointed to the island that was our destination. It appeared surreal in its haunting beauty, with its first-growth cedars growing moss beards, standing sentinels, as if assigned to keep watch over unwelcome intruders.

As we navigated towards shore, I could see a figure scurrying between the shrubs and trees. I jumped out before the boat was fully anchored, calling Jonathan's name. Further in, I detected what appeared to be a plastic greenhouse tucked away, with no other habitation in sight. Jack reminded me that I had less than two hours before he had to head back.

During that time I attempted to persuade Jonathan to come home, but at the suggestion, his body tensed like a bristling cat preparing for resistance. He wasn't going back to a place where he would be expected to be what he is not, he said.

For the third time, Jack pointed to his watch, but I needed to spend further time with Jonathan. After bargaining back and forth, Jonathan offered to take me back in his skiff, docked on the beach, and Jack left.

The ocean before us stretched into infinity. A couple of eagles soared leisurely overhead, keeping watch over their territory, while Jonathan gazed into the distance and said. "They never found him."

"Who's they?"

"The R.C.M.P., they never found him."

It turned out that another squatter, whose name was Brian, had joined him. At the mention of the name, Jonathan began to fidget and a frown clouded his face. It turned out that Brian had found a human skull among the underbrush of salal.

Having spent time at Peg's wilderness resort, surrounded by first-growth cedars groves, I was aware that the native population of this area had buried their dead in the trees; therefore, finding a skull was not uncommon. When Brian returned with the skull, I found out, it suddenly transformed into a blood-soaked apparition of a native woman, screeching at them in rage, while Brian kept running in a circle, likewise screaming. The following morning, he disappeared and was never seen again.

We sat silently for a while then prepared for Jonathan to transport me back. With the low tide, the skiff sat firmly moored. Jonathan unloaded the fuel tank and lifted the motor out in preparation to pull the boat across the mudflats. I found a pair of oversized rubber boots. The one boot had a gash, and with each step, the hole greedily sucked in the mud, delaying my progress.

Finally, we dragged the boat to bob on the water and Jonathan walked back for the fuel tank and the motor. After we boarded, I removed the boot, rinsed off the mud, letting the chilly evening air dry my foot. The next task was to use a tin can at hand to bail the water seeping through the crack in the hull.

Back at the cottage that night I was kept awake by the haunting story of the apparition and by the chill of the room. A tree had hit the power line, depriving the bedrooms of heat. When I mentioned Brian's name, Peg confirmed that the R.C.M.P. during that time were indeed looking for a missing person like him.

In the morning, Peg announced that she was driving into the village as she called Tofino and asked if I wanted to come along? I decided to stay. "I will continue to keep my ears tuned in and keep you posted," Peg said.

"I really appreciate your help, Peg."

I walked outside and burrowed my toes in the sand. Nature has always been my solace, and I hope will be preserved for the following generations to enjoy.

GOOF'S HOMESTEAD

JONATHAN eventually left his island hideout and moved back home. But later on, he disappeared once more. This time, according to Peg's detective work, into a trailer on someone's land.

I loaded the car, filled the gas tank and set out for another trip across the winding road over the mountains. On my arrival, dear Peg in her usual way comforted me with her silence.

In the morning, I started the car and followed the directions I'd been given that led over an old bumpy logging road, with the occasional deer leaping across. I saw a black bear with two cubs serenely grazing on the bank. Occasionally, I stopped to consult the instructions, until I came to a sign that said GOOF'S HOMESTEAD. I drove through the gate then turned off the ignition in front of the house. It was built from beach-combed logs and driftwood.

A man stepped out of the house. "What can I do you for?" he asked.

"I am looking for my son, Jonathan. I was told he lives here."

He pointed straight ahead. "In the clearing."

I looked around.

"You can leave the car here and follow that path."

Towards the end of the path, an eerie feeling tingled through my body. Ahead, at the incline of a hill, stood two replicas of the cabooses that were shown to me during my delivery and later depicted in my coffee cup, which I was told to push up the hill if my baby and I were to survive. But these here were no mere apparitions.

Goof appeared, offering to knock on Jonathan's door. I composed myself just as Jonathan stepped out of the first caboose. His handsome face looked thin and gaunt, and my mother urge longed to take him home, run a hot bath and cook his favourite meal for him.

Later, I mentally connected with the priestess shown in the cup, inquiring about our association, and why the pushing seemingly hadn't ended yet? What was the answer to that message?

Although I have partly made it up the hill, it isn't over yet because I have not completely liberated myself from the association, I am told. As for the message: It was a prediction that mine and Jonathan's journey won't be easy; and her connection, had always been part of my personality and the co-writer of my book. Through me, she had chosen to experience the earthly suffering of those who succumb to its darkness. This however no longer has to continue but it is time to step outside, become my awakened self and embrace the possibilities. The following day while strolling through an art gallery downtown, I saw a painting of a lily. Upon closer inspection, its calyx looked like a dilated vagina in preparation to give birth. This symbol of birth means connecting with myself.

DEATH, THE GREAT CLEANSER

THE following were the words I spoke into the wind as I tossed Pau's ashes into the sea.

And so it is, that we say goodbye, but not for the final time. The regrets of the should" and the "should-not-haves" in time will dissolve by the power of the special gift of each other, glowing in intensity in the memories of the stars.

Although Pau and I were separated, towards the end when he was admitted to the hospice, I would regularly visit and sit by his bedside, holding his hand in mine, the presence of death being the great cleanser. His once magnificent body looked so unbelievably frail. I could see how he appreciated my visits and chose to be touched. But at what point did we switch to a diet that failed to nourish us?

Now as I sat at his bedside and we reminisced about our travelling days and our unforgettable adventure through the Northern wilderness before the complexities of our personalities interfered, I recalled when Pau tripped while carrying me across the threshold on our wedding day and we landed on the floor in a heap of tulle and satin. He showed his infectious grin that always made me laugh and said, "You look scrumptiously delicious."

WAR CHILD

A Time For Grieving

> *"Violence as a way of gaining*
> *power is being camouflaged*
> *under the guise of tradition, national*
> *honour [and] national security."*
>
> **ALFRED ADLER**

TODAY I received a letter from Australia. It's from my childhood friend Anna, informing me that she is planning on a visit, next spring. It's Remembrance Day. As I passed the statue of the fallen soldier at the cenotaph, I grieved for our own fathers. They were also no doubt good soldiers in defending their country and loving their family – as is every soldiers duty, but received no recognition for a job likewise well done even though they had fought as hard as the other side. They were executed in the fields, most of them never formally buried nor immortalized on a memorial list of honour. It was simply a matter of nationality and of either being on the losing or winning side.

Late summer 1944

During that period, unbeknownst to anyone, Anna and I would visit the soldiers entrenched in underground hobbit bunkers camouflaged with shrubs and other vegetation. With benches and tables sculptured from the ground, some of the tables had bouquets of flowers arranged in bottles, and stoves pushed chimney pipes through a hole. Handsome young men and boys – our heroes, surrounding our community in a defensive ring to protect us against the raiding Partisans. We enjoyed singing alpine Lieder (songs) together, and other catchy tunes.

Then one day there was a battle and the bunker habitations were reduced to piles of rubble. When we arrived, an eerie silence reigned. It was hard to associate these mutilated dead bodies with their staring lustreless eyes, to the beautiful vibrant young men and boys of yesterday whose mothers I imagined were waiting for this war to end, and for them to come home. Not knowing that the death of warfare had already claimed their lives, and there was no one to gently close their eyes. No loving hand to stroke their brow to ease the transition. Nor a grave marking their existence.

Anna and I stood transfixed amidst this horror, our stomachs retching up blobs of vomit from our mouths, until our brain signalled our feet to run.

When we arrived back in the community, the streets were swept clean of life, with everyone barricaded behind doors holding their breath, lest they drew attention. Only rumours prevailed – the heralds of uncertainties. Some of these rumours instilled hope while others were too frightening and had to be brushed aside.

Soon after, Anna and her mother relocated to her uncle Herr Baumann's house, where they expected more protection and from there, our fate took us in different directions.

DREAM

THIS past memory surged forward to the present, expressing its self through a dream the young Leni had kept on hold for the adult Leni to unravel in the present.

In the first part of the dream, a canopy of ominous clouds cast grey shadows over a dreary set of buildings enclosed by a high fence. A long column of stooped bodies. Their eyes in a state of shock, trudge through one of the gates.

Upon entering the building, a cast-iron box catches my attention. It turns out to be an oven with a glass door turned black from smoke, left slightly open. A naked male body is crammed inside, his face hidden behind a metal overlap, where each second must be an eternity of searing pain. I understand that what I am facing, is an interruption of his execution placed on hold by sorting us new arrivals. He seems familiar, I know we have met before. I leave the group and walk over. I want him to feel my presence, whisper, "good bye." I try to form the words, but they won't cross my lips, they remain internalized in a silent scream. Even if he would reply I realize, I couldn't bear the sound of the tortured voice probably gone mad from pain.

I try to catch a glimpse of the executioner's face but it is turned the other way.

When later we meet, I am surprised at his unremarkable appearance, looking like someone's uncle next door.

It's obvious we are in a camp. We follow the routine and surprisingly are provided with adequate food and showering facilities. Yet, I feel there is a sense of deception here, a pretense of a simulated security, to keep us manageably docile.

KATHARINA NOLLA

"Please, tell me the truth. When?" I ask the executioner whose face I can now clearly see.

He seems surprised by my question. I realize that he doesn't have the answer either. His job is to merely take orders.

The dream shifts to a second stage. I am still an inmate, but now a cancer patient. Two nurses appear. One is carrying a reclining seat with a baby strapped in. She says to the other, "There is no point to intervene. Let the situation take its course." They turn and walk away. An inmate clad in an immaculate white suit is cheerfully walking down the hallway. "Why are you in denial?" I scream at the top of my voice. It must have scattered the demons of the night. "There is a war going on, spreading cancer, with babies strapped away, left to die – and you are pretending all this is normal!"

Next, we are assembled in a large hall, facing a stage where the camp personnel are rigidly standing at attention amidst a silence awaiting a verdict, with all movements conducted in slow motion. My eyes try to communicate with the executioner, but he is on official duty, standing at attention in a posture as if dipped in a starch solution. ...Victims all, including the executioner.

It is clear that the dream was activated in response to the memory of the massacre Anna and I had witnessed. What were the symbols trying to convey?

The young man in the oven definitely represents all sons devoured by the abyss of war whose mothers are waiting for them to come safely home.

The executioner's job is to follow orders unquestionably. Blind obedience is the key to success in the theatre of war.

What is war supposed to teach us? We so compulsively recreate over and over again. What is this great lesson even 'peaceful' countries send their troops to participate? How many more have to be repeated where unaccountable lives continue to be sacrificed? Dreams turn into nightmares and make the transition of death an experience of horror rather than a peaceful passage.

This period in my memory from the latter part of 1944, lurks as a state of ongoing derailment with desolation along its tracks, stripped of everything that felt warm and precious. I can certainly identify with the bombed-out victims of the current war-torn regions, again calling out, "please understand!"

...Understand that this is not a movie, and the nightmares will continue to haunt the generations.

The victims deprived of their home, miss the laughter and sweet labour, where they dreamed their children's future.

Humiliated, living in bleak conditions, under such circumstances even an otherwise passive personality could be provoked to retaliate by inflicting what was done unto them.

If their children's survival is threatened, it should be understood that they would unite at any cost.

At the cost, of blowing a hole into the universe even though they would rather swap vegetables with their neighbour across the fence.

Why should anyone be surprised at the thought of retaliatory action, reciprocating terrorism for terrorism, from those who crack from the overload.

Jonathan

DAY PASS

I received a call from Itak to meet her in the square where Saul-Paul used to hang out. When she arrived, she looked upset because the news channel showed beautiful young men and women in uniform killing each other, she said, and children being maimed and terrorized by invading soldiers kicking down the doors of their homes. She was referring to the prolonged Iraq invasion, which mother declared as an additional period of dark history of long-term effect. "Why are they doing this to each other?"

"They are soldiers and are told they are at war."

"War, against what, or whom?"

"It's about rooting out terror."

"I don't understand. How can you root out terror with terror? Are your soldiers at war too?"

"Some are participating in it, although it's waged in another country far away, called Iraq."

She looked confused and said she didn't understand because she couldn't see evidence of any invasion that called for a counter-invasion.

"The rationality is to weaken their power, and show a display of force to discourage them from invading ours," I explained. I reminded her that according to her story their planet was in a similar situation once, therefore she should understand. She pointed out that she was referring to their pre-planetary shift and that she is a post shift generation. "But now, as I look around, I am experiencing our past through your emerging present," she added.

She paused, and asked, "How about meeting in the sacred space. Don't you have a sacred space?"

When I had no answer, she told me the story of their great teacher named Ot who played his flute on the rooftops. It was always the same plaintive tune, with an overtone of humming sounds, "Yes, it can be done…" The tune made everyone who heard it feel good and peaceful. Gradually, others adopted and played it to each other. When someone felt upset or angry or had difficulty falling asleep, they played it. When children cried, they played the tune until the entire population practised and joined in. Ot expanded his territory by playing at the entrance of schools and churches, in front of shops and theatres and the parliament buildings. Eventually he dared to play his instrument in front of the arsenals that stored the weapons while he ducked the bullets aimed at him, over and over. Yes, it can be done.

He crossed the border into neighbouring countries and the people welcomed him, until there were no borders remaining. One day the entire population united, rushed toward the arsenals and dismantled the weapons.

That became the sacred place.

Embracing each other with tears in their eyes and joy in their hearts, it was said that those on crutches threw them away and danced, and even those who couldn't hold a tune sang, until the planet vibrated with joyous celebration.

The delicious aroma of food drifted from the restaurant across the street, and I suggested we get something to eat. I was surprised to discover that Itak, although occupying a human body, only eats one meal a day and as I observed, in moderate amounts.

"What are your Idrisian caloric requirements?" I asked.

Prior to the transformational shift from the old anxiety-ridden period to the new period, their population required an intake equal to ours, she said. But now it was twice a week.

"Bathroom?"

"Also twice a week," she laughed.

Lehni

WAR CHILD CONTINUED – THE AFTERMATH

THREE years after the war, Anna suddenly stood at our door, released from the camp with its history still censored by the world.

When we looked into each other's eyes, something that should have been present and celebrated with juvenile jubilation was buried under deep layers of scars no surgical procedure could remove and silenced by the years in-between.

The child Anna I had known, prone to plumpness with a complexion that looked like the skin of a fuzzy ripe peach, now appeared pathetically pale and thin. I so longed to pamper her with a steaming bath she could sink into with a sigh, and see her giggle as she once did. I wanted to present her with a delicious feast, but all I could offer was a dish of potatoes prepared with exhaustive ingenuity.

As I looked over the·stark reality of our squalid accommodation, I recalled the spacious rooms with their high ceilings in the house at Berak. The lush fields yielded an abundance of fruit and vegetables. The smoked hams and sausages hung from the rafters, watermelons and fresh yogurt were stacked in the cool cellar on a hot day. I didn't miss the look of disappointment on Anna's face at the sight of our shabby surroundings and tried to avert my eyes from the sight of her threadbare dress patched under the arms. At that moment, I felt powerless and resentful at fate's betrayal and perceived poverty as an act of punishment.

Before settling down for the night, Mother said, "Poor child, all alone without a mother, who will take care of you?"

"We will take care of her," I said.

She crowded in with us, sharing my bed.

Jonathan

PEACE

ACCORDING to the church, as long as we continue to pray, God will deliver. If this is so, then why have the answers for peace so far eluded us, I ask my Maker.

They also serve as a ladder for climbing up the way to heaven, but at times the ladder will veer over and collapse.

"Why have the prayers for peace so far eluded us?" I ask.

"You distract yourself with ongoing disputes. But then just as a solution seems viable you stack them on your mental shelf and then ruminate some more. The answer is beyond words but requires practice, and no one else can do this for you.

Keep your hands off each other's territory until you have no need of territory.

Your world likes to categorize peace with the symbol of the dove. Occasionally, great discoveries have been pushed into reality but when it comes to the concept of war versus peace, you have lost perspective.

Remain connected with yourself and each other. Practice the law of sharing instead and celebrate your differences, then dance until you dance no longer but soar."

Leni

THE SACRED

SEVERAL days ago after a meditation retreat and before drifting off to sleep that night, I had a vision of a lady dressed in a brocade Byzantine gown, kneeling beside my bed. She held out a beautifully wrapped box for me, which I understood contained a message but I felt I had to decline the offer because I didn't feel evolved enough to honour the sacredness I knew it contained.

Weeks later when she appeared again, I still had to decline.

But last night, after I bolted from a disturbing dream, gasping for air, I said, "I am ready."

When she held out the box once more, I had a flash of insight into what it must contain. Instead of untying the ribbon, I asked her to untie it for me.

As the box opened, I couldn't stop laughing, because I realized that this was the gift I had prayed and wished for all along.

As I suspected, the box was empty.

The gift of emptiness; it is a space devoid of judgment where I can find myself and love myself. It's a place where I no longer have to strive for what I think I am lacking. Judgment no longer has a place to hide, and God resides; my cells sing to one another. It's a place from where I can send my intellect on vacation and become aware of my awareness. A little voice said, "And don't just think, but listen, here you will discover yourself."

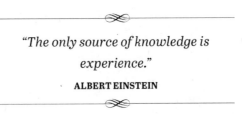

"The only source of knowledge is experience."

ALBERT EINSTEIN

For years, I have been a seeker. Have I found what I have been seeking? Perhaps I will arrive at my goal the moment I stop the seeking. That doesn't mean I should underestimate my thinking mind. It has its organizational skills and its vast storage space to house the data that can be of use. On the other hand, it seems that the primary breakthroughs and discoveries are manifested during my non-thinking states.

I give gratitude to my family, who were my teachers, even though many days at times seemed to be treated as unpleasant chores where airing seldom took place and passion shrivelled like prematurely dried leaves. At the same time this environment awakened in me the vow that I will at no time allow my own passion for life to be diminished, nor stand in the way of completing my lessons.

"The last moment of my life then will be the happiest of all – the final reward," I said to Ida, "coming as it will with the relief that I don't have to participate in this striving and seeking any longer but celebrate my arrival.

What the world needs is one huge splash of a global party! For an entire month each year all weapons should be laid to rest to celebrate our planet and one another. After all, what would life be without the opportunity of discovering ourselves in each other?

During this time, I imagine jets to be on standby free of charge for the bushman of the Kalahari, the forest tribes from the Amazon, the striving New Yorkers and fashionable Parisians. Trains and buses, boats, helicopters and private cars would offer sightseeing tours. Posters announce free accommodation while everyone would be blown away by the discovery what had been considered impossible has become reality, already planning for the next event.

Just think what this kind of environment would do for the children carrying such an amazing legacy of trust into their future, and the money saved to create equality for all.

"Let's party."

Jonathan

I am recovering from an injured knee. The ward is settling down for the night. In the distance, the light of the beacon is projecting a streak of red across the water. The moon hangs at an angle, looking through the window. Our nurse walks in and draws the curtains across, then walks out.

I ring the bell. Stan, the nurse assistant pops his head through the door. I ask if he would pull the curtain back the way it was.

"What's the problem?"

"I was just going to have a conversation with the moon and now the curtain is shutting him out. I think he wants company."

He pulls the curtain just wide enough for moon to show his face again.

Before closing the door, he says, "I'll be back later after you've had your conversation with your friend. Ask him to shine brightly – I have a date after the shift," and he walks away laughing.

MESSAGES FROM THE MOON

It's just as I thought. The moon admits to being lonely. There was a time when humans believed he had something to contribute, he tells me sadly. Now, the focus is primarily on scientific equations. No, this is not as straightforward a job as it once was, he says. There was a time when the forces synchronized, now the connection has weakened, the coordination is not what it used to be, its leadership is in chaos. The elements are crashing out of control and its muscles have lost resilience.

"This planet of yours, it used to be such a happy place once, but now ... sometimes you get good tenants and other times not so good. Yes, poor buddy Earth is now suffering from anxiety and constipation most of the time, belching and coughing, the bowels are slack and the respiratory tract is not so good.

He proceeds to quote the verse from. Ecclesiastes 3: 1-8: in the bible

There is a time to be born and a time to die,
a time to plant and a time to uproot,
a time to kill and a time to heal,
a time to tear down and a time to build,
a time to weep and a time to laugh,
a time to mourn and a time to dance,
a time to scatter stones and a time to gather them,
a time to embrace and a time to refrain from embracing, time to search and a time to give up,
a time to keep and a time to throw away,
a time to tear and a time to mend,
a time to be silent and a time to speak,
a time me to love and a time to hate,
a time for war and a time for peace.

"By the way," Moon continues, "you can tell Stan that I am not some kind of fortune teller. I have my own agenda, but he can send a warning to Nurse Nocturna to mind the lawnmower cord in her patio. I suggest she unplug it if she doesn't want to trip."

"What about those legendary scars that are attributed to your crust of skin?" I ask.

"They are the results of the rough-neck tenants that came and went."

"They weren't by chance our previous ancestors?"

"Let's leave it at that."

In the morning, Stan is back. He looks at me and says, "Your nurse buddy won't be in tonight. She tripped on her lawnmower cord and now she's in bed nursing her knee."

Leni

SUCH PRETTY BLOND HAIR (THE GREAT CLEANSER)

THE city is enveloped in mist of fog. It's the kind of mood that inspires a sense of introspection. I am sorting through Pau's Escher-like sketches, through the ribbons and trophies he won for his swimming and diving competitions before he drifted into depression. As for his personal biography, he left behind a scant portfolio to piece his past together. The only childhood story he shared with me was how he used to drop in at his parents' store after school. The customer ladies would coo, "Que guapo" (how handsome) and admire his blond hair, then such a rarity before the influx of tourism from the North and the peroxide on the shelves. He told me how much he hated their comments and how he would mess his hair in defiance. He briefly mentioned that his father had been interned in a concentration camp during the Spanish civil war, and often there hadn't been enough food to go around. I encouraged him to talk about it. But I soon learned that there was little room for negotiation when it concerned subjects connected with his past.

During the last weeks of his life, while I visited him in the hospice as he lay dying from cancer, we connected on a level that had previously eluded us.

I would quietly sit at the edge of his bed holding his hand and offer him sips of freshly squeezed juice. He would dutifully take a sip or two while drifting in and out of consciousness. It occurred to me that this was ultimately the kind of relationship he always craved for – straightforward simplicity.

He used to say that I was too complex and that further words merely added to the complexities. Now sitting at his bedside, his life reduced to the bare necessities, these past arguments seemed trivial as we sat at the threshold of where life and death meet, devoid of pretence. Is this the final prize, the great cleanser, when the moment of summation shrinks to fit into the tiniest capsule to be presented to God the Creator?

At the end, when he seemed over-medicated, restlessly pulling at his covers while uttering a mix of Catalan and English, with intermittent mutterings of "No, no," and then some cursing, and something about "He is lying in the ditch," and then more "No, no." A story unfolded, in which I could make out a priest had played a role.

"Pau, what's going on?" I asked, and in a voice hoarse from exhaustion he uttered, "He took my power away." Then his eyes flew open like an unhinged door, his gown was drenched with perspiration, and there was terror in his eyes.

"Pau, what is it, who took your power away?"

His eyes stared into space.

"Pau, tell me what you didn't tell me before."

It turned out that one day during the civil war, as he walked along the street he saw a dead body lying in the ditch. It was his uncle's. His child body shut down

KATHARINA NOLLA

overwhelmed by this indescribable horror. As young as he was, one thing was clear to him, judging from the adults' whispers he had overheard, as well as his own observations – that you were not to tell anyone what you saw in such a case. If you did, you were going to implicate the rest of the family and they would be rounded up as collaborators.

He walked the streets instead of going to the store as he normally did and passed a church with the door open. He walked in and sat on a bench, too numb to cry.

It was peaceful in there. A priest came out to light the candles and the boy wondered if he should dare to confide in him. But he didn't know whose side the priest was on. Nobody knew whose side anyone was on and even children were aware of this. The priest came over and smiling, slid onto the bench beside him, asking why the sad face and admiring his hair. "From whose side did you inherit this beautiful blond hair," he asked.

The child turned away.

"You are so shy! Don't be afraid, I am just going to touch your hair."

The child placed his hand over his head.

"Tell me, where do you live?"

Afraid, the child gave him a false address then suddenly began to shiver.

"Poor chiquet, you need something hot to drink. Come, let me take you to the sacristy to take care of you."

He prepared a cup of hot cocoa and placed some bread and a piece of chocolate on a plate. "Now tell me about yourself." When Pau remained silent, the priest said, "Que preciosa, look, you are still shivering," then he slid close and placed his arm around him and with his other hand he guided the child's hand to his crotch that felt as hard as a stick. His eyes had an unnatural gleam in them.

"Oh Pau," I said, cradling him in my arms, his body now so unbelievably frail. It did what I had never seen it do – shiver without resistance – and my heart rejoiced at the sight of his release. He didn't have to stick his finger down his throat to release the stuckness, as I was prone to say.

When I visited him the following day, he smiled with that spark in his eyes that lit up when he felt at ease. "Remember our vacation on Maui?" he asked.

I smiled and nodded.

"When we were invited to that party and you wore your white Goddess gown that draped down to your feet. And when afterwards we drove along the cane fields you took your shoes off and tossed them to the back seat, asking me to stop because you wanted to make physical contact with the soil?"

"I remember."

"Then you ran through the field with your laughter trailing behind you and the stars sparkling in the sky, calling for me to join you, and afterwards we waded through the outgoing tide to rinse the volcanic soil off our feet, and you looked so beautiful and I said, "Let's make love. And you said this gown is too complicated.""

Yes, I remember. I took it off and then it floated out to sea and Pau jumped in to retrieve it, and of course it was dripping wet and we laughed, and I asked, "Now what will I do?" As an answer he handed me his shirt, which of course was also wet, and I ran to the car with nothing on, and before I reached for Pau's jacket from the back seat, another car pulled in and we drove off.

It's these spontaneous moments when we stepped out of the way and allowed our playfulness to take over that had kept our marriage alive as long as it did. It takes so little, just a bit of recognition and we become as pliable as candle wax. It's this kind of fragility that makes us so preciously human.

Everything seems fine, and then one day it isn't. Yesterday on my way home from doing errands I passed a church along the way. A bride floated across the lawn in front – a vision of radiant loveliness in a cloud of tulle and satin, with her groom at her side, both laughing on the way to the limousine as the guests pelted them with rice. I asked, why has this experience been denied to some? But this time, no answer came through.

The story isn't over yet, I consoled myself. One chapter ends, another unfolds, at times with a surprising new twist. Simply setting foot on this planet is one huge venture. A world where the impossible becomes possible and I leave myself open to a myriad of possibilities.

I am my world. It's when I neglect my spirit to a point where I don't even show up on the screen, I pile up a history filled with rubble, viewed as failed opportunities and chunks of years wasted that my world gives no credit for.

But there is also great courage in taking on challenges that seem to lead nowhere, which force me to examine the situation from alternate angles with the possibility of new discoveries.

I am the world I am waiting for. I am the mystery to explore the bits and pieces of this gift to myself – a personality like no other. It's so excitingly volatile becoming the wanderer, the storyteller, the crone, the prince and princess or the fairy godmother wielding the magic wand.

Jonathan

AFTER a concert in the park, as we sat by the ocean, with the waves splashing against the shore in rhythmic movements and the moon admiring its reflection, Itak in answer to my question explained that contrary to our earth bodies, their Idrisian bodies are no longer regulated by a hormonal drive as they once were.

"Then what motivates the desire for procreation?"

"When a couple share a special moment in a deep sense of infinite spiritual communion, their energy like the stars burst into particles of co-creation."

"Like a Big Bang?"

"Something like that."

"But now you are in this earthly body."

"I know what you mean," she said. "

We gazed out at the sparkling moonlit sea.

"Will the earthly hormones kick in to be activated?"

After she thought about this, she replied, "That, I cannot answer."

I wondered how Hira would be judged for his deception on his return.

"Judgement is a form of stagnation, while the universal law only recognizes transformation."

"How about those who break the law, whom we consider criminals – do they exist on your planet?"

"Our motto is 'let each be heard so that all will be heard.' The feeling of exclusion no longer plays a part on our planet. Therefore, the word "criminal" has been struck from our vocabulary. Should one of us stray and lose direction, support will always be present to guide us back into balance."

Next, she quoted Ot their great teacher who played the flute that catalysed the shift: "God Creator does not wait behind doors in a surprise attack by wielding a rod of punishment as some preachers claim. He seeks out those who have gone astray, to lead them back home."

"What happened to the rest of your crew?"

"That I don't know."

"You haven't by chance run into them?"

"Let me remind you, my dear friend, that they could have integrated in any part of your globe and manifested in any H-type race or nationality." She reached out and embraced me, and it felt good.

Leni

ODE TO CREATION

I look at nature's magnificent sustainability. I am part of this wondrous dance that the universe has toiled through millennia to integrate into its choreography of perfection. It's when I fail to surrender to life's embrace that I drift out of balance.

The miracle is that even when I step out of synch, my innate technology is designed to patiently guide me back to re-join in its dance, all with single-minded and loving attention. How much reassurance do I need? How much proof is required before I can shed my doubts that lead to separation?

There is only one way to reciprocate in this tremendous co-ordination and that is by honouring its infinite creation, and one another, of which we are a part.

At times I have messed up and admittedly a bit of tarnishing occurred, but then there is nothing some polishing can't restore. I have to remind myself that God must have meant what He said on the seventh day when he looked upon his work and expressed his contentment. He was pleased with his creation. I can do great things as well, to the point of stabilizing my own world when it seems to wobble on its axis.

On the other hand, how will He deal with me when it's time to empty my pockets and strip for inspection, and it appears obvious that I have not entirely fulfilled my lessons?

As an answer, I am shown a vision of the other side, a preview of what will be waiting at my arrival. The veil is lifted and there is my beloved Creator. I bow to His presence, ready to kiss the cuff of His sleeve.

He reaches for my hand and, lifting me up gently, he says, "Look."

As I turn, magnificent fireworks explode across the celestial sky accompanied by exquisite sounds that send shivers up my spine.

He smiles. "It's these moments of your return that inspire the celebration."

I feel humble, knowing that it is only when I doubt myself that I feel unworthy.

"I had no idea," I say, awed by this exquisitely wondrous partnership, knowing that I am loved.

Next, I find myself lining up on stage with the other new arrivals; we are the stars of the moment. The trumpets are blowing, the angels are ready, eagerly waiting to hear our earthly stories that I understand are a continual source of fascination to them. Our guides are ready to greet us, as they were always ready and in the background, my familiar soul friends who appeared in my out-of-body experience are excitedly waving.

Back in the present, I am inspired to write the following words that flowed from my pen:

Worlds collapse then intertwine, the cells tell their stories. The self will vanish then return with renewed fresh thoughts of insights beyond what the eyes can see. I get up to kiss my grave from where I will always resurrect.

COMING HOME

"No bird soars too high, if he soars on his own wings."

WILLIAM BLAKE

THERE is an aspect of myself that is overly-protective of my emotional energy, huddling away in fear of myself. Frantically searching for the answers, I can't deliver.

It seems that I have examined my emotional pain from every angle. Like the clockmaker's apprentice who has to dismantle the clock to understand its mechanism, I too need to examine the mechanism of my own components. When I feel out of balance spinning in a murky fog, I must remind myself that this might be a cloudy day, which will not last forever. The longing of coming home is a longing to connect with myself. When I am looking for this elusive self I will look for it in the reflection of others, while they are busy looking for their own reflection. There is always the option of escaping into my stillness. In this state, I tap into my knowing. When I discover the cause of my suffering, it no longer seems as overwhelming. I recognize it in others and healing will allow the neglected love to shine through. I still hold the conviction that we humans have the capacity to transcend beyond holding dominion over one another which results in war and material inequality; and I see the light of hope is still alive.

I have just returned from a ten-day retreat. In my absence, Jonathan stayed in a little guesthouse belonging to a Vietnamese immigrant named Mimi. There I met her helper, a chubby cheerful girl named Linda who would remind Jonathan of the daily schedule. "It's video night, Jonathan, I hope you will come!" Or "Don't miss tomorrow's picnic, Jonathan," and he would rouse himself from his isolation and join in. I found out that her birthday is coming up and Jonathan, who doesn't remember mine, actually marked hers on the calendar and took note that she likes cheesecake, and I noticed that she wears ribbons in her hair.

A VISIT FROM THE PAST

THE Japanese cherry trees lining the boulevards are at their peak performance displaying their blossoms. Vendors, artists, jugglers and musicians claim sections on the causeway, while the magnificent horses harnessed to the decked-out carriages proudly strut through the streets. Pedicab drivers draw attention to the local points of interest to tourists reclining in their seats like visiting royalty. In the harbour, flotillas of whale watching boats are heading out to sea.

I am on my way to the airport to pick up Anna who is arriving from Australia. After we departed for different continents, we corresponded, then for a while lost touch.

She suggested that for quick identification I should wear a green scarf and she green shoes. I didn't know what to expect. The last photos were exchanged way back, with her "kornblumenblaue" eyes sparkling from the photo. Kornblumenblau was a song with a catchy tune, serenading a beloved's cornflower blue eyes, which we used to sing while we marched through the fields on our way to visit the soldiers in their underground hobbit dwellings.

The passengers are streaming into the lounge with their eyes blinking at the sunshine. A group of Japanese tourists chat excitedly, with their cameras aimed to click, a man wearing a cowboy hat has a Calgary Stampede sticker on his carry-on luggage. Then, the green shoes show up and a pair of shapely legs.

After a brief scan, we run towards each other with our arms spread out like a pair of hens flapping their wings.

In the car, as the years flash through my head and countries have re-charted their borders and acquired new names, all I can think to say is: "How was your flight?"

She nods and smiles and I smile back, our eyes filled with awe and wonder that here we are – us. In the background slumbers our history with a childhood interrupted. The missing pieces of the puzzle now falling back into place.

We are no longer mere fictitious beings, but Leni and Anna. An excitement flares up with the realization that I was a little girl once and here sitting beside me was the link to that past, the only link.

Sitting in my home, cuddling into the intimacy of sharing our morning coffee, I ask, "How long has it been?"

"The last time was at the dance near the village when you canoodled with that cute boy you recently met who had a crush on you, both of you looking sweet and innocent."

"Oh my goodness no, I mean yes, there was this innocence once, so completely trusting, then. What was the word you used?"

"Canoodle. The Austrians call it kuschln."

"Oh, cuddling." How could I have forgotten that first experience with the two of us snuggling up like two puppies? But too many changes were happening, and it was after mother's death, and the plan of immigration was hastily taking shape to leave the past behind. I recall the disappointment in his eyes at the news, while in my head the raw energy of that far-away country across the ocean beckoned.

Life had that kind of flavour once, shrouded in mysteries still in the making. Other memories are waiting to be unpacked from Anna's suitcases.

"Life at times seems so boringly predictable," Anna observes, "but on the other hand, had someone predicted that our history would play itself out on opposite continents – one in Australia, the other in Canada – who would have believed it then? When I look back now, the past seems like someone else's story."

She reflects on this and then says, "I know this is changing the subject. I can see how involved you get in the news, of what's going on over there right now. Personally, I don't care what they do. Let them kill each other if they want. That's what they seem best at, making sljivovic and at intervals massacring each other."

Looking out of the window, she says, "Remember when we sat in the meadow and I talked about the camp? I never talked to anyone about it again. Who could have related anyway, or cared to know? Instead I made up my mind that I was going to have fun and no one was going to snatch this privilege away from me again." Absentmindedly rotating the cup in her saucer, she asks, "How about you, did you meet your Mountie? I remember when you read your first book in English, it was about a girl who married a Mountie and they moved to the freezing North where they travelled by dog sleigh. That's why you chose Calgary as your destination, because you thought that's where the Mounties were stationed and from where they kept law and order among the wild characters who settled there. So how did you end up marrying a Spaniard – a Spaniard, in the freezing North?"

"It could get pretty cold up there," I joke, "and I needed someone to keep my feet warm."

"Didn't they have hot water bottles up there?"

"Not a comparable substitute."

"Do you believe in karma? Morgan believed in karma."

"Morgan?"

"My second husband," then she surprised me by mentioning the young soldiers entrenched in the bunkers. "Massacred, some were just kids no more than seventeen."

"What about Morgan and his karma?"

"Whenever I worried about him, he would laugh and say, why worry? When the time is up it's up and you go. He was a race-car driver. Then one day he crashed – karma."

"Oh Anna, what a shock it must have been!"

"Let's clear the table and get dressed. I want to go shopping and you have to show me around."

The translucent glass of the lamps along the dining room walls reflects mellow light beams through the room. Our waitress looks like Mortitia from the Addams family, blending with the antique furniture. Absent-mindedly twirling her wineglass, spilling some of its contents, Anna is watching the customers come and go, and then she faces me. "How often do you have to go through this?" She is referring to Jonathan's absences. "And where does he go?"

"Mostly 'under the bridge' – a hangout the locals call the place. It's an abandoned packing plant located at the bank of the bridge, were as he says, he doesn't have to be who he is not.

"Is it safe? Who goes there?"

"Mainly street people."

"Aren't you worried? I mean someone in his state, being out there, how can you let him?"

"Dear Anna, he is six feet two! Do I look strong enough to sling him over my shoulder and dump him into the car?"

"Where does he shower during these periods?"

"He doesn't."

"How do you cope? I can hear his pacing at night, that must keep you awake."

Again: What am I expected to answer.

"I am the mother."

"How about when you need a holiday?"

"At times I arrange for him to stay at a little guest house."

"How about travelling?"

"I haven't done that since my trip to the Middle-East."

During the stroll after dinner, we passed a building with a door partly open and music drifting out.

"Tango," Anna said excitedly. "Morgan and I belonged to a Tango club. Let's go inside and check it out."

Couples of various ages undulated across the floor and soon we too were invited but I felt too self-conscious. It had been years since I had stepped on a dance floor.

My eyes followed Anna's feet gliding past the table, first with one partner, and then another.

"Come on, get up, join the celebration," she called in passing. "Show off your trim figure."

"No, I am out of practice." Pau had not been into dancing, but sports.

She returned with a drink in her hand: "For you."

The notes of the music teased and caressed and soon my own feet were gliding across the floor, locked in the embrace of confident arms firmly guiding me, evoking memories and my body wanted more and I continued to dance.

On the way home we laughed and I felt shamelessly silly and reckless. I suddenly swerved and barely missed another car, furiously honking.

"Oh my God, that was Elsie from the Vitamin shop. I hope she didn't recognize me," I said.

And then we laughed again.

"That was fun, yesterday," Anna said. "What's on the agenda for tomorrow?"

"What would you like to do?"

"Well, certainly not looking at another totem pole sticking its tongue out at me." She referred to our visit to the indigenous museum.

"Let's make a reservation for that seaside resort I told you about and on our way home we could stop at the sweat lodge on the native reserve."

"A sweat, why should I want to sweat?" she laughed.

"Because I am invited, and I would like you to come."

The smoke from the pit spirals towards the sky while a breeze playfully tugs at my skirt and caresses my skin.

From the distance, shrill calls signal a flock of Canada geese approaching. Bursting into an explosion of chatter, they flap their wings overhead propelling themselves in the direction of the marshland nearby, perhaps on their way to keep a rendezvous for lunch. A deer leaps across the meadow, nearby.

In the pit, the rocks have acquired the right temperature, ready to receive our offerings of tobacco before entering the lodge, which some First Nations people call "the womb of mother earth."

Inside, sitting in a circle on the floor lined with layers of cedar boughs, we silently watch the rocks being arranged in ceremonial succession, gulping for air in reaction to the initial burst of steam from the rocks assaulting our lungs. The ancestral spirits are evoked. At the sounds of the drumming, the chanting voices speed up and the outside reality begins to fade.

At intervals, the sounds come to an abrupt halt with only the exhalation of our breath sweeping through the silence, then they burst forth in a crescendo that threatens to rip the tent apart.

During a long pause, we hear weeping, the sighs of release. "All our relations."

Gradually our bodies begin to shift then re-adjust, the flap of the tent is lifted and all eyes blink back to the daylight reality. Still in a daze, one by one, we crawl through the opening and head towards the house.

In the native tradition, no ceremony is complete without "the sharing of food." It never fails to amaze me the sacredness the food acquires in this atmosphere steeped in silence – that, I call a true communion. I can feel this sacredness wrapped around the trees, nourishing the grass, saturating the soil, body and spirit.

Inside the house, I join the circle on the floor next to Anna whose eyes stare into space, her skin a waxy texture.

"How are you doing," I ask.

"Can we go now? I will tell you later, on our way back."

Night descended on our way home, winding over a stretch of mountain range enveloped in sleepy serenity while the trees floating alongside gazed back in silence. The only sounds were the hypnagogic swishing of the tires and Anna's breath rising and falling as she huddled in her seat. "It's so dark," she said. "When you find a safe spot I would like you to stop."

I turned off at the next lookout spot ahead with a view of the fjord below and silenced the engine, while Anna slumped further into her seat, her arms hugging her chest.

"Are you cold?"

"I am bloody freezing."

I grabbed the blanket from the back seat and she gratefully wrapped around herself. "Something happened during the ceremony in that tent," she said. "I saw Mother's eyes that looked like two black pits in that wasted face back in the camp, and her stick-like arms reaching out to me for comfort, as she did then."

I reached out and drew her close, while her eyes pleaded with mine. "And do you know what I did?"

Her hands covered her mouth, stifling the words, a flood of sobs poured out as she averted her face. We clung to each other.

"I looked the other way, instead, because at that moment, I couldn't bear to face that pitiful pile of rags that used to be my beautiful mother."

"I understand," I say.

"I don't know if you do, I don't think anyone does. She begged for comfort, but something shut down inside of me. The lights went out."

I sat immobilized, engulfed by this past crashing back, then with both of us rocking back and forth and Anna screaming, "I never forgave myself, I don't think I ever can," before she collapsed with exhaustion.

"And no one ever asked us," she said quietly.

"Asked what?"

"No one asked to hear our stories.

"And just when you are about to relax with the memories tucked away, life presents moments for them to sneak back out again."

I said what I thought most of us usually would in memory of a departed to comfort the living. "Your mother is in a better place now, Anna."

"How do you know?" she demanded. "Maybe she is infused with anger like I am! Maybe that's why my marriages didn't work out and I am being punished. The truth is that I feel guilty for having greedily sucked at life and survived, while she didn't."

A breeze drifted through the window that caused Anna to sink deeper into her blanket. The clouds dispersed, the moon sailed across the sky casting a silvery patch on the fjord below while we stared into the night, silently clinging to each other.

Another memory surfaced: The day her once beautiful proud mother slipped and fell on the way to the latrine. Two guards stood nearby and while Anna rushed to her mother's side, trying to save her dignity, they laughed and made filthy remarks as they pointed to her mother's worn panties while she lay sprawled in a dirty puddle with her skirt bunched up. If she could have gotten hold of a gun at that moment, she said, she would have blown their brains out to erase their twisted laughter, why is anybody surprised at terrorism? Don't they get it?"

She told me how in the early morning hours the limp bodies were collected, heaved onto trucks, and those alive were enslaved to cultivate the fields from dawn to dusk to feed the nation. There were young mothers whose children watched them leave in the morning and eagerly waited for them to return with the hope of a crust of bread, or anything edible they could scrounge at the risk of being whipped.

"Demoralize the enemy from within by surprise, terror, sabotage, assassination. This is the war of the future."

ADOLF HITLER

Why am I telling these stories, some might ask? That already sound like the lowest level of pornography?

The answer is that I vowed early to one day expose this ongoing cycle of humankind's great deception. Repeatedly inflicted against one another under the pretence to be fought for the sake of peace. Currently accelerated by a technology and irresponsible leadership now capable of immobilizing this planet that is our home to a nuclear winter if we are unwilling to change.

On the other hand, let this be a reminder that we are also blessed with a sacred centre, and are the recipients of free will.

Anna has boarded the plane. Seated in my car in the airport parking lot, with the memory of her body shivering against mine as we sat in the dark on the mountain, I could feel my chest tighten. In my mind I saw it encased in armour that reminded me of the shell of an armadillo, which had been shielding me from a memory now threatening to crash through. I doubled over to protect myself, but too late. I tossed and turned that night, haunted by the experiences that had piled up in rapid succession. There are periods when you erect a wall around your emotions. You know they are there because the pain is real, but your mind and brain need a break. When Anna and I sat in the meadow near the old farmhouse after her release from the camp and she initially told me her story, there were no tears to be ¹shed. Neither on my part, nor hers. At Mother's funeral, I couldn't cry. And children grow into adulthood and some will be unable to cope with the overload in their heads, but in desperation might curl their finger around the trigger of a gun or any means available. Or become parents one day, and what stories will they have to tell their children?

"You have to come for a visit, Leni," Anna said on the way to the airport.

"I will and I'll bring Jonathan along," I promised.

At this, Anna fell silent and looked out the window. Then she said, "I couldn't, Leni. I just couldn't take the disruption of his nightly pacing. I hope you understand."

"I understand," I said, but I felt sad.

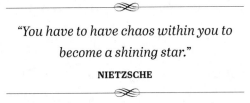

"You have to have chaos within you to become a shining star."

NIETZSCHE

There are days that fail to work out as I think they should, perceived as failure, even when abundance is staring me in the face, I deprive myself of its rewards. Might that perhaps have something to do with me standing in the way of progress?

When I stray from my path, I become disconnected from myself, missing out on full participation. Each sliver of self-inflicted deprivation gives a message of scarcity. How then can life support me when I disrupt its rhythm?

Life should be a mutual affair. My first step should be to introduce myself to myself. To spend time with myself, experience this me. I am after all, my number one investment.

Take care of your body. It's the only place you have to live.

JIM ROHN

A voice stirs within, confronting me with a question: "Leni, will you join yourself in marriage?"

I laugh. "Join myself in marriage, frankly, I don't think that would s a good idea, since I am not always that easy to be around and get along with."

"Give it at least a try."

I hesitate.

"Do it."

"Okay, I will."

"Then repeat the words of your marriage vows."

"All right. I, Leni Almador, promise to take me Leni Amador as my lawful wedded spouse in marriage."

"To honour and obey until death do us part."

"I am not good at obeying, but I will agree to honour."

"To have and hold from this day forward in sickness and in health, for richer and poorer?"

"Yes."

"Then say it."

"To have and hold from this day forward for richer or poorer, in sickness and in physical and mental health."

"How about love and cherish?"

"To love and to cherish until the day this body falls apart."

ANNA'S SECRET

THE day before her flight back as Anna and I sat on the front steps, she revealed a secret she had kept hidden away throughout the years.

After the camps closed over three years after the war was declared over, its former inmates were still barred from the job market, reduced to working in exchange for food or a corner to sleep in. One day when Anna had no place to stay and while walking through the street, she was in desperate need to relieve herself. She walked into an eating-place and asked if she could use their toilet. The younger male customers looked her over and evidently guessed her background. "Njemci nisu dovoleni," (no Germans allowed) they said, and laughed at her.

She walked out. In desperation, she squatted in a nearby alley. Then she heard the snickering voices and this moment of humiliation clung to her like a slimy layer that she will always associate with squalor. Her eyes widened in terror as they looked into mine. "And you know what," she continued, "when Rod's, my first husband's business failed, it evoked the same terror I associated with that past moment. Thereafter, I was sure to attract financially successful men who would protect me against such circumstances."

She searched my face for a reaction then said, "Isn't this the most selfish exploitation you can think of?"

"I am sure you loved him," I answered.

We silently stared off into space. Then I turned to her. "Did you love him?"

Her expression of fear vanished. "Yes, I loved him," and she reached out and squeezed my hand. "Thanks for being with me," she said.

"Thanks for being with me, too."

Practise being good to your so-called enemy, I said to myself, even those locked behind bars; be sure to treat them kindly.

As long as war remains on the human agenda, it requires victims – and it could be you or your children added on the list one day.

After hours of accompanying Anna on her shopping expedition, and sitting on the steps too long, my bladder now called for attention. I got up and walked into the house, with Anna following behind.

WHERE DO THE MOMENTS ESCAPE?

IT poured last night, a storm whipped through the trees and two of them must have leaned over, slamming against each other, sounding like giant footsteps. The waning moon paid me a visit. I tried to count the fading stars then drifted back to sleep.

When I woke up, the sun's rays filtered through the branches, dispersing shafts of gold. The sea looked smooth and satiny, with silver stars flashing on its surface. Across the shore, the mountains were covered in strips of fleecy clouds, behind which I imagined nymphs might be taking their morning baths. A cargo ship chugged into the distance. eagles and cormorants flew their errands, while the cottage standing on the cliff gazed serenely out to sea. A school of whales honoured me by announcing their presence in passing.

After Jonathan's diagnosis, I would come out here to gorge on my mother guilt, wallowing in self-pity. When I was sated with my past, I gorged on the imaginary outcome of the future. Yet my true personality longs to burst out and explore the other universes that show up, with a lookout post from which to observe the world outside.

At times, I want to drift off to indulge in an imaginary life where Jonathan's position had turned out otherwise. But out of respect for him, I decline to go there, since it might imply that he is incomplete. "Am I to blame for Jonathan's condition?" I ask again.

This time I receive the following reply. "When you walk through the desert, it seems vast and unproductive. But look closely and tears will come to your eyes at the revelation of its beauty. Understand that you are each other's teachers; therefore, be generous in your intentions."

"And then when the lesson is complete, we die?"

"Death is a word of your own conception and indicates annihilation. In the eternal design, there is no death. For essentially it is all about spirit. At times you neglect this spirit and allow it to become caked with impurities. But when you expose it to the light, the layers will dry and crumble, exposing its brilliance. Then it not only reconnects with you, but integrates with all dimensions.

Now when I come out here, surrounded by nature's magnificence, I slip into nothingness and discover my playfulness. In its moments of simplicity life attains this kind of elegance.

Jonathan

IT'S the season of golden rain. That's what mother calls it, when the tall poplar trees in our backyard shed their golden leaves, dancing down from heaven. Its edges look like filigree jewellery covering the yard, glowing in the twilight.

Mother is laughing the way she used to, when life was young and innocent, as she picks up a bunch she tosses in the air. Before going back inside, she scoops up another bunch, which she then drops into a bowl. I know these leaves carry a special meaning for her. She had told me about the trees that had lined her father's estate and how the ground was covered in layers of gold each fall. But when she took me there, she looked sad, because the land appeared neglected and stripped of its spirit.

Lehni

TWO STORIES

THE second time I visited the country of my birth I located Uncle Ivica. He was living in a cramped little apartment in Osijek, Slavonia's capital. People used to say of him, "Look at the sparks of fire in Ivica's eyes." But now his warrior body stood before me with its shoulders stooped like a fighter whose spirit had suffered disillusion. The city appeared constrained in subdued drabness and lack of self-expression after years of watchful totalitarianism. I rented a car and we drove along the coast. On our way back we passed the depressing co-op building with its corrugated roof, which had replaced the stately house of Berak. We asked permission to look around. There were still traces of the orchard. We came upon a cherry tree, loaded with my favourite fruit. As I reached out to taste their summer sweetness, I recalled how even out here, with the beautiful spacious grounds, mother would isolate herself in her room. But one afternoon she stepped out and appeared standing on the stairs, beckoning me to join her. When I entered the sitting room, she pointed to the radio and motioned for me to sit on her lap and, with her arms around me, we listened to the music flowing from the ornate box in front of us.

THE POOR NEGLECTED CHILD

My home in Victoria, BC

DURING a workshop on the subject of motherhood, a lady whispered, "My mother wasn't kind to me."

Did I consider my own mother had lacked kindness towards me, I wondered? I recalled her words echoing back from the past in response to my own, spitting from my adolescent mouth. It was in response to her frequent statement that all she wanted was to lie down and die.

While I spilled out my frustrations by pointing out that each of us had to eventually take charge of our own lives, to complete our assignment.

She said, "how can you be so disrespectful to your mother." Then reminded me of the difficult baby I was. When all I did was cry and refuse to eat. In retrospect, I concluded that she couldn't give me more than she had to give, as she couldn't give herself what she lacked. At the same time, it occurred to me what a challenging task it must have been for her, to deal with this scrawny wailing creature she had given birth to, while simultaneously she was faced in protecting her mother from the violent outbursts of her abusive husband.

Now back to standing under the cherry tree with the dawning realization that out here at Berak was the only time I could recall my mother's arms around me, I could write two stories about this. The first story could be approached from a psychological analysis, while I craved for more, spilling this fact all over the place for everyone to see, pointing to a neglectful childhood.

A second memory emerged. It was a hot summer's day in Austria. As mother and I walked through the village in search of food, we crossed a road covered with fine dust. Suddenly, mother bent down and when she straightened, she pulled out her hankie and wiped tenderly at what she held between her fingers. Then, with a smile reminiscent of the afternoon at Berak she handed me a cherry, gleaming like a jewel in the sun. I remember savouring the tiny bites to prolong its juicy sweetness while basking in the love of that special bond that flows between a mother and her child. In further retrospect, I perceive these experiences like this: In their rarity, these moments stand out with special intensity, and yes, I could have craved for more. On the other hand, it only takes one moment of an encircling arm or a cherry in the dust to be unwrapped with the memory retrieved for the bonding to be carried into eternity. In the end connect with our wholeness like the thief on Jesus's right hanging on the cross, in the end after taunting and belittling Jesus's intent, also connected to the moment of wholeness.

UNCLE IVICA'S VISIT CONTINUED

I slept on his overstuffed couch. We went for walks and sat on park benches, reflecting on our history.

"It wasn't easy for any of us, and there were scant choices in its complexities," Uncle Ivica said after I questioned him about his own earlier past. "When one is young it is easy to become aroused by a passionate ideology with its conviction to serve the good of one's nation, or whatever one identifies with."

"How about blowing up bridges? Were you involved in that?"

"It's the rule of warfare."

His wife, Katica, whom I had not met was off visiting relatives in her village. When she came back, we hugged and stood back to look each other over with pleasure. She cried and I could feel my own unreleased tears but didn't know why. Was it the regret of having missed the time to enjoy and celebrate each other, wasted by a concept called war and nationality, class barriers and political outlook between the families, while the spirit longs for the simplicity of sharing?

I approached the most painful subject, Oma's last days. It was Uncle Ivica who had managed to smuggle the information across to us about the heart attack.

"How did she die? I mean was she in a safe environment, did she linger on?" I asked.

His eyes filled with compassion as he silently gazed back into mine. "She was safe, and I think she was too exhausted to linger."

I told him how I would check every newly arrived train and refugee trek, repeatedly asking, "Have you seen my Oma? Her name is Teresia Pilli."

I asked him about the people who had rescued mother and me. "Who were they and how, in that line of stooped bodies, were they able to identify us?"

"You wouldn't remember the car that crossed the line as you trudged along a road near Valpovo. I sat inside with my cap pulled low. That's when I pointed out your mother, grandmother and you to the others in the car."

"There must have been certain risks involved for those people."

"We were all at risk. Had we been found out no time would have been wasted in stringing us up as collaborators."

The past rumours were true then. Uncle Ivica had joined the Partisans.

"I can understand your loyalty as a relative and there are no words that can express my gratitude and acknowledge your bravery, but what was in it for the others?"

Too many unpleasant memories have been kept alive, but there were also the others. I don't know if you remember your mother worrying about your father becoming too implicated with certain refugees? They weren't merely refugees and mountain men from one particular side, but simply people who needed help. Your father, being in the Wehrmacht with certain connections, had access to help where others couldn't. He also took great risks."

Yes, I did recall the gaunt faces of the mountain men and other unexplained visitors walking away with bags of grain and of father coming home one day with a grim expression. He had just arrived from the railway station and he spoke of cattle cars with stick arms dangling from between the bars of the windows in the stifling heat, begging for water. Father found a bucket and a ladle he passed around in spite of the warnings from the nervous soldiers standing guard and I understood there were other people like father who weren't afraid to become involved.

Later, as I walked through the park where I found a secluded bench, my thoughts drifted back to my immigrant friend Alex, in Calgary, also a war child. While sharing our experiences one day, Alex surprised me by asking, "Had there been a choice, would you have asked to bypass this destiny?"

My reaction was a jolt of surprise at such an odd question while my lips simultaneously uttered a prompt "No."

After all, as long as wars are being waged, there will be victims – and why not me? Only as a victim I can reveal war's impact to the world – and thereby hopefully contribute to awakening its consciousness. Something else occurred to me: (But I do not necessarily recommend – unless one is prepared for it.) Being on the losing side makes war seem less enticing to participate, and adds a touch of humility.

Back in the present, I reflect on my mother's ultimate bravery in her last days when her mould-infected lungs filled with fluid, and her wheezing voice instructed me to see the seamstress in the adjacent town, because she wanted the best for me. I should be properly dressed for her funeral. Her main concern was to hang on until the dress was ready and her child would be respectfully attired for the occasion and I knew she loved me. It was a moment beyond crying and I recalled the voice that had asked me, "Are you prepared to enter into the sacred?"

And this was part of the sacred.

Jonathan

YESTERDAY I met Itak in the park. She looked sad. "I miss my home, Jonathan," she said. "Now I understand the meaning of your word 'alien,' and the concept of exclusion. I am an alien in an alien world."

I didn't know what to say because I am not used to dealing with emotions, especially not in consoling an Idrisian female in a human body. The situation is already complicated as it is and some of us humans are aliens too, unable to deal with our present system.

"Do you believe in asking for divine help?" I ask.

"Your planet is known for its temptations that digress from the evolutionary path," she said. "We were warned about this and much debriefing will be required on our return. Your ancient Egyptians were fond of painting the single eye. The eye of God, some historians tell you. But we know it represents the eye of the inner self that keeps its silent score. And yes, we do believe that help will never be refused. But to quote Ot, "Merely praying for help will have no effect as long as my hands are rummaging through another's pocket.""

Leni

AN INSIGHT INTO MY TRAUMA OF CONCUSSION

THIS morning as I stacked the lawn chairs in my garden shed, I accidentally hit my forehead against a steel post. I got up and stumbled to the nearby clinic from where I was sent to emergency.

On the way, with the ambulance careening through the streets, I had a chance to observe my amygdala in the emotional fight and flight limbic system frantically ringing its alarm bells into action. My initial reaction was to shove the commotion of this overzealous organ out of the way in order to quieten things down. Yet, as I soon discovered, this was easier said than done. Like my ego, my amygdala likewise insists on its pre-tested position and will not readily relinquish its post.

Some dialogue needed to be exchanged.

"Dear amygdala, I began, I respect your position and know you have a job to do, but now that you have made your point by alerting the entire household into action, understand that I also have a job to do." Having said that, provided a degree of calmness and I decided we could work together.

Next, I observed my analytical intellect, deciding to check things out, adding further complications to the situation. One thing was clear: I have a thick skull. I slid my hand across my forehead and marvelled at the magical encasement that has withstood this hard bang by protecting the hierarchy of my brain.

Shortly, healing pulsations began to stir and I expressed my gratitude for the tremendous intricate components the universe had invested in me and that I so callously take for granted.

After the test results, I was sent home with an order to rest.

Reclining on my living room couch, it became clear that resting is a foreign concept to me, which is likely why I got into trouble in the first place. The flowerbed in the front yard needs weeding, the shrubs against the fence to be clipped and soon I was bustling around in my usual routine.

The neo-cortex in my brain kicked in, scowling, letting me know that I was interfering with its job to sort things out. Since I didn't follow its advice, it had to do what it had to do. It simply decided to check out. From there on, my morning hours were encased in a misty fog, floating in a trance of disconnectedness.

When at noon the fog began to lift, my nervous system reacted with jitters of agitation. It rebelled against the imposition of being forced to deal with the everyday responsibilities, while the ego asserted its position. Sending the ego on vacation actually felt quite pleasant, I found, and I asked why no one had warned me about all this before checking out of emergency?

CRYSTAL LIGHT HEALING

NEXT, I treated myself to a crystal light healing session. During this deep meditative state, two apparitions clad in white gowns bent over me. Surgery was discussed and I found myself drifting into a blissful state of what I can only describe as cosmic anaesthesia.

When I woke up and drifted back into the present, I knew there was a message in store. Before the next client slipped through the door I asked for permission to remain in the empty waiting room to jot down the messages I knew were waiting.

This was the message: Know that all is taken care of. It always was, and always is, and you will have full access to yourself and be mindful not to interfere in the process. Trust yourself and trust in our support. We understand that trust so far has been a challenging concept for you, but all that you need to know and do will come to you.

True, yours has not been an easy journey, but know that this no longer needs to be. Relax into the journey and it will be long and prosperous. Partake of the fruit paradise has to offer and taste its sweetness.

Do not long for what does not belong to you but embrace the journey. We understand your challenges for we were there once and have been groomed to become helpers and for that you can equally prepare yourself.

Jonathan

"THERE is so much I fail to understand," Itak said as she leafed through an old magazine of the Rich and the Famous.

Pointing at the first photo, she asked, "How many of your population live in such buildings compared to the tiny dwellings?"

"My guess is maybe one percent."

Then she pointed to the photo of Buckingham Palace and its acres of manicured grounds. "Who lives in this, and what portion do its residents occupy?"

"This one in particular belongs to the Royal Family of England ... and they occupy the entire estate – grounds and dwellings."

"This must require many hours for them to maintain."

"It doesn't, they have others do the maintaining for them. By the way, how many of your own population live in such style. "Our land is not divided off into parcels of real estate like yours, and such places as depicted in the magazine exist yes, but no one will occupy a portion larger than they can maintain for their personal use."

"How about your ruling class? What kind of lifestyle do they expect?"

"The answer is that we all take joy in sharing. Should one fail to find a suitable spot, a consultation takes place and the vision becomes reality."

Then her gesture clearly indicated a loss of interest and we moved to the next block where we listened to a band.

KATHARINA NOLLA

Leni

THE PIRLGRIMAGE OF
THE HUMAN JOURNEY

IT leads through moments of despair, tears and laughter. It is an experience where betrayal and greed show their faces; hate and violence stare from the pain of separation. Yet likewise love and compassion play a role. Yes, so much love that often goes unrecognized when the messages are unclear and I imagine God gazing down, saying, "Look, no matter how foolishly they behave at times, and how their lack of faith in their own knowing leads them astray, you have to love them for their bravery taking on this experience."

How can I synchronize the present with the past? The past written in stone while the present appears as fleeting moments difficult to capture and the cells are assigned as record keepers of the script.

THE VAULT

JONATHAN is still ruminating about the possibility of entering the vault he imagines contains his manual.

"What do you expect to find in it?" I ask.

"The other me."

"What would that look like?"

"Where I am no longer expected to think like everyone else."

Shrouds of fog are rolling in from the ocean, enveloping the world in a veil of mist. I light the logs in the fireplace that crackle to life.

Fairytale characters' wave magic wands to make things happen. Legendary masters supposedly tap into laws the rest of us have little confidence to try.

Shamans claim to have travelled to the moon from where they returned with mysterious objects as evidence.

After Tati's death, I found solace in spending time with the cows and horses resting in their stalls, mimicking their breaths, which induced a hypnagogic state far removed from the world of war and violence. As then, so now I allow my breath to take charge, inviting Jonathan to join me.

Soon the outer world begins to fade, replaced by a gently swishing sound reminiscent of a sweeping broom, followed by an ocean of silence.

Contrary to my previous out-of-body experience when I ascended through a tunnel of light, Jonathan and I are sucked through a dark tube. Gradually all movements cease and we step out on hard ground marked with cracks, facing a door a short distance away. There is no building attached, nor a wall – just this one door in the middle of nowhere.

The surroundings a natural barrier. The door is locked, we soon find out. Jonathan takes charge by wandering around while I decide to stay behind.

Next, I am startled by the sounds of footsteps, the door creaks, then opens. A man of undefinable age clad in a shabby suit steps out, scrutinizing me with hostile eyes.

"You are intruding on private territory," I say.

We stare at each other.

"How so, if this is your territory as you claim, then why haven't you taken an interest in checking in before now?"

"And who are you," I ask.

"I am Wodon, and you should know how some of us feel about negligent landlords that suddenly barge in.

Such disrespect will not go unnoticed.

After all, when you abandon your territory, you can expect squatters to move in."

He is standing inside my comfort zone and his breath has an unpleasant smell. As I look around for Jonathan's support, my alarm bells activate my concern. Jonathan is nowhere to be seen. After calling his name aimed in all directions, his voice faintly calls back, "I am searching for the key!"

Wodon reaches inside his pocket and with a smirk on his face tauntingly dangles a key.

After Jonathan's return, and at his request, Wodon surprisingly hands over the key and follows us through the door that automatically shuts behind us. Once inside,

Wodon smugly dangles a second key. "The exit key" he notes. I panic at the possibility of being held hostage in this dreary environment. Stacks of scrolls are piled on shelves. A cursory glance reveals some isolated words of wisdom, but mostly they are scribbles of worn-out doctrines, political and religious rhetoric and decrepit theories.

Wodon, who is leaning against the doorpost with his arms folded, sarcastically remarks, "Not very impressive information is it? But then, what can one expect? They are the human imprints of your mind."

The left corner of this cheerless space, accommodates a large stage. From behind a curtain, a row of bodies stream forth, some, heading in my direction. I understand they represent our human emotions. In this case, primarily in feminine gender, craving for attention.

"Welcome our award-winning dancer, Shashaya," a commentator announces, while from the stage Shashaya clad in a robe of many colours, makes her entrance, waving and throwing kisses to the audience who enthusiastically clap a welcome, and the representatives of emotions surround me. Whispers of comments are exchanged.

The first arrival, clad in a green blouse and a wraparound skirt of the same colour, begins to scowl and fidget, looking about her. Then suddenly rushes back towards the stage creaming, "Award-winning indeed, it should be me standing up there!" She accuses the judge of corruption. From a basket she is carrying, she pelts what look like rotten pears at the dancer, splashing over her dress, while the audience boos and pelts back the squished pears and then drag her out of the door. I see the word Envy stitched on the hem of her skirt, while already a new arrival vies for my attention. Wodon warns me that should there be interviews, they have to be brief before Jonathan's and my time runs out, again jingling the exit key.

The next arrival stooped in a dejected attitude, is wearing a shabby grey robe, pleading for help.

"How can I help?" I ask.

"It just won't go away."

"What is it that won't go away?"

"This unbearable discomfort. Wherever I go it clings to me and no one seems happy in my presence. They call me Misery." I realize that each arrival expects me to get involved by participating in their drama – they represent the human drama, although I would rather look the other way. Instead I admit that I can identify with her plight.

"And you weren't embarrassed by my association?"

"Believe you me, your presence no doubt caused its share of anxiety, I associated with weakness, while I pretended to be strong and deprived myself of the sweetness life has to offer."

"Can you help me?"

"I can help you in the way I helped myself."

"And that is?"

"By the conviction that I have the power to transform my personality to a more manageable aspect and refine my thinking, it will improve my digestive system too."

"That means, I can find relief too?"

"You are the collaborator in your story who can negotiate alternate ways that suit you."

At my suggestion, she smiles and dances away singing the words: "I can do it too, I can do it..."

"But it's so lonely in here," a new voice butts in.

"Who are you, and why are you lonely?"

"What an embarrassment, I have heard my family say, referring to me as a product of Failure."

"I sympathize and can definitely identify with its symptoms: The low self-esteem and depression I experienced through my financial collapse, and battling with my maternal guilt."

"What was your solution?"

"To ask if this is really the kind of company I want to keep and the investments to choose, reminding myself that alternate opportunities are available."

The next drawing my attention is a male figure clad in a red cape, aggressively striding towards me. He is definitely not a welcome sight. I avert my eyes in the hope that he will go away.

"Don't pretend you don't know who I am," he demands.

I decide not to get drawn into the confrontation but then realize he will not leave until I admit to the truth.

Yes, we have met. It was on my way home from school when he tried to recruit me to join his legions. His name is Hate.

Once I confess to the association his desire to hang around no longer seems as pressing, and he walks away.

The following arrival needs no introduction as she dances towards me decked out with garlands of flowers and stars sparkling in her hair. I reach out to grasp her hands and can't mistake the joy reflected in her eyes. I long to bask in her presence, but the occasion is cut short by Wodon arriving with Envy at his side, once more reminding me that only he is in control of the exit key.

Just then, Jonathan who had veered off on his personal

pursuits has returned. Wodon points at the bulge under Jonathan's shirt and asks Envy to investigate. Envy retrieves the bulge, which turns out to be a worn manuscript.

"Were you trying to sneak these out?" Wodon fumes at Jonathan. "Someone call for the Inquisition!"

Shortly, two Wodon look-alikes arrive and promptly drag Jonathan away with his hands tied behind his back.

"They were to be destroyed with the rest of the pile during the fires of Alexandria," Wodon continues to fume.

I panic. What if the door were permanently locked, holding us hostage never to return back home?

The two Wodon look-alikes drag Jonathan beyond hearing distance, kicking him to the ground. But Jonathan manages to pull himself up to face Wodon who looks back in surprise.

Being too far away, I can't make out what Jonathan is saying, but Wodon suddenly bursts out laughing. The other two join in, slapping each other on the shoulders while Jonathan turns in my direction and seems to wink.

"What did you say?" I ask Jonathan on his return.

"I invited him for a visit once we get back."

"And what did he say?"

"He said they have a saying around here: Beware of Humans." Then as an afterthought he added, "On the other hand, I might just take you up on that. It gets pretty crowded in here at times,"

"What were you trying to sneak out?"

"Too bad it didn't work. It contained some speculation about a future portal shif."

Shortly, there was another commotion and the exit door slid open.

THE HEART OF THE COSMOS

IT was after my Tati's funeral, that I found myself floating through the tunnel of light. At the end of the tunnel two apparitions clad in white gowns pulsated waves of love, waited for me. I had finally arrived back home, I rejoiced.

To my disappointment, they gently shook their heads, indicating not yet. But this was where I longed to stay, my wish begged to be granted. As an answer, they once again shook their heads, giving me to understand that what I was shown was merely a preliminary example to my final hour, that there is more than my eyes can see, but that my journey wasn't over yet.

"All right then," I said and waved at them as I floated towards the tunnel on my way back to my earthly home. At that they smiled and nodded. For two weeks after my return, it seemed that my feet defied the pull of gravity and I floated above ground, embracing the memory of their loving presence.

Again, I told no one about my experience that instilled in me a confidence to look for short cuts beyond earthly limitations and into the heart of the cosmos. I believe it is the creative principle that has been driving evolution from the beginning of time. With the conviction that should I at times fall back into moments of despair, I must remind myself that I am part of this eternal force. And I can rest assured that regardless of the religious affiliation God is perceived in, he does not scourge his domain with a whip in hand to punish those with pertinent questions on their lips. I express myself in interaction with my fellow travellers. We hand each other platters of experiences and my willingness to taste from these platters depends on my degree of curiosity and my sense of adventure. Should I occasionally mess up, I must not regret my mistakes but celebrate my courage that embraces these experiences. After all, what would I learn by shutting myself behind doors where the air turns stale and my mind stagnant, to pollute my head?

Sadly, some of us refuse to understand that nature's gifts are to be shared instead of sticking on price tags of entitlement.

LIFE IS A SERIES OF SEASONAL EXPRESSIONS

WHEN I separate myself from myself I drift through a fog of concepts, stuffing the briefcase I carry, filled with fickle abstracts, without commitment. At the end of my days I could hand over the contents to the next generation, extolling its merits. They initially might reject them, but in a moment of complacency and lack of trust in their own knowing, might pick up the worn generational pages after all.

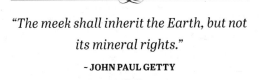

"The meek shall inherit the Earth, but not its mineral rights."

- JOHN PAUL GETTY

Nature is a series of seasonal expressions and will not defy its own law. At the end of the season the leaves on the tree won't suddenly announce: "This coming season I will defy the wind from blowing me down." Or decide to hoard the water for its sole consumption and pile the nutrients around its roots to cause a shortage for others.

I am life once I realize I am life, which can be a scary concept because I am forced to participate.

Let nature be my teacher, nature practises true economics; it doesn't waste, it is us humans, who lack this insight. Until this kind of imbalance becomes a confinement in its lack of participation. Therefore, I must remind myself that at no time am I excluded from this infinite cycle. The waves of the oceans washing ashore, the mountains keeping watch over the valleys below, the rivers carving their beds – and that I must not support any administration that squanders and depletes this treasury. Once I surrender my administration into someone else's hands, I am again left with abstracts, associating with others holding briefcases of abstracts that at the end of the day are already obsolete. While the following day yet another administration might try to convince me to buy its shares, screaming from the posters along the highway. Until one day I realize that I have lost track of the contents of my own briefcase and as I study the pages, I find the information already obsolete. I toss them out to be scattered by the wind and I am free of these pages devoid of passion.

So here is a reminder to myself: That whenever I become distracted and remove myself from my own partnership, I must not shift blame on others – nor point to the good old days before the resources were depleted and there was still enough food to go around and plenty of water running from the taps. The health care system had something to offer, the highways still led somewhere and the children had a place to play. But admit to my own irresponsibility and should ask where I had been, when I could have made a difference, instead of confined in my inaction.

Perhaps people need governments to mutter their complaints in its ears. Governments need oppositions to transfer the blame and distract the population from the truth.

THE RECORD KEEPER
MY FRIEND — THE ROCK

ROCKS are the historical record keepers. Once you befriend and gain their trust, they will share their stories. Maybe history is written in stone, after all. The following narrative, related by my friend, the Rock, explains it well.

The story dates back to a climate of perpetual spring. A time of seeding and cultivating, blossoms, buzzing bees and chirping birds. Hatching and birthing churned in an ongoing cycle of celebration. On the beach, Undal and his tribe of two-leggeds had settled. They gave birth and honoured the souls of the dead.

All was calm and peaceful as they picked the fruit, nuts, the roots, the leaves and all the food that was pleasing to them. The music of their voices mingling with their laughter indicated a sense of joy and of playfulness.

One day, an unfamiliar sound shattered their routine, followed by deep rumbling from beneath the ground. On the ground sprawled a spectacle their eyes had never seen before: a twisted face lay in a sticky pool of blood, dripping into the soil. The spirit of the ground went into shock.

They had just witnessed the first homicide, motivated by greed and power competing over the collective source. Earth cried out, its voice reaching the heavens. The ground froze over.

From then on, sheets of ice covered their world and most of the land creatures perished. Rumours had it that

Undal and some of his tribe managed to head southward and survived. When the warm winds swept in to melt the ice, it was obvious that most of the sea creatures survived as they swam close to shore, bringing their babies to the edge, while others acquired the habit of laying their eggs in the sand.

Decades later, Undal and his tribe returned. They had now acquired the need for meat, hunting the animals for food. "At night, we watched them dance around flames of fire they had learned to harness," said my rock companion. "These performances usually took place after a successful hunt. But the wildest celebration followed after one tribe's victorious raid over another. By then, they coveted what the next one had – although there was plenty to go around when they didn't resort to waste, nor destroy what they fought over.

"The rest – as you know my friend – is history repeating itself. But now it's on a large scale, never before imagined, crowding each other out."

Night is settling in, a wind whipping the branches of the surrounding trees and sweeping across the rock, and I bid a good night.

On the way down, I ruminate over what I had been told, and wonder if the message has been totally clarified.

I turn around and climb back up.

"What's next," I ask, "what direction is in store?"

"It's not my job to be preachy, but frankly, with your shaky leadership in power, even us in our rock solidity are concerned."

"Large-scale tribalism, divided into 'countries', competing with each other no longer serves you. Your technology has become too destructive, poised on alert position aimed at each other.

"As a collective, you are all in this together. A lesson unlearned, will only haunt you, until you take the responsibility to get it right. Ask yourselves, 'What other home will you have to go to? What other body, to inherit? What memories take to your grave to comfort you?' No one else can do this for you."

"Good night," I bid again. As I walk back down in the dark of the night.

Leni

THE POSSIBILITY OF FINDING TREASURE UNDER THE LID

THERE were moments when I imagined I had found the answer to my questions. My cluttered slate wiped clean and time became irrelevant. At other times panic sets in when I feel the years escape too rapidly and the enormity of life scares me, looming as such a huge affair where I want to move mountains, but feel so small. It is as if I am an apprentice looking for short cuts to mastery, forgetting that my practicum has barely begun. Patience is not one of my virtues I must admit, and my sense of direction needs improvement.

As for Jonathan's condition, I have attended Shamanic ceremonies and even considered exorcism to minimize his diagnosis. "Do you believe in all this?" my friends ask. I tell them never to underestimate a mother's determination to tread where others failed to venture. "Schizophrenics have no coping skills." How often have I heard this and at times have even agreed with their observation?

No coping skills? How would I adjust to living in their colony? It would certainly set my head spinning. And that's okay as well. Then on and on I go, as Pau said, peeking under the lids of the crocks along the way. There always remains the possibility of finding a treasure under the lid of the crocks, or a teacher might appear with the answer, and the questioning period never needs to end.

A true teacher will not slam the door in my face and I must remind myself that the same should apply to my inner teacher, myself. By now I have rummaged for so long that I am used to the smell of compost under the lids because at my core I am a "peasant" and familiar with compost. In the long run, when everyone else has left and Rome has crumbled, it's the peasant who knows how to work and rebuild the soil. So, the story never ends but leads back to the soil and the peasant, who throughout history has carried the physical load on his or her back, now replaced by the middle class, carrying the load of taxes in place of bricks?

THE FIXER

I have just returned from an afternoon of running errands and find Jonathan looking for a piece of tape, babbling something about a bird with wounded wings trapped in the garden shed. The telephone rings. It's my friend Ida on the line. I tell her to hang on while I look for a roll of tape and Jonathan calms down.

When I pick up the phone again, Ida is crying. It's over some relationship-related problem concerning her daughter, at least as far as I can make out. When she tried to help, her daughter screamed, "I told you before not to fix things for me. Why can't you leave it at that, can't you get it?"

After consoling Ida and seeing Jonathan settled, I hang up and examine this word, turning it from side to side as if it were a tool I hold in my hands.

Fixing: I can understand the daughter's feeling of invasion and identify with the mother's rejection while both yearn for the warmth of appreciation.

We mothers don't give up easily. I can envision Ida stoically marching equipped with various tools strapped to her skirt – tools suggested by other mother braves who vouch for their success.

Ida called back. They had a talk, she told me. Actually, first they screamed and then talked, she said. I again consider this word, "fixing" and ask myself if the word were a tool, would I agree to stoop down and admit that I need fixing?

Jonathan

THE year is winding to completion, ready to step aside for the new Millennium to take over. "What will the new have to offer and what are its predictions?" I ask my Maker.

This is the answer: The Millennium is yours, you are the creator of the predictions; therefore, be aware of your planet that is calling, reminding you to respect the creatures in the sky, the earth and the sea. Sadly, as a collective species engrossed in your self-indulgent complacency you shut out their cry and their weeping in the night. You have become such noisemakers that you can no longer hear each other, but even tune out the self while racing with your technology attached to your ears detached from nature. Earth is a parent with the priority of its children in mind; it has given you much but lately has suffered greatly and needs to be nurtured back to health.

Leni

A CHILDHOOD PAST – EAST OF EDEN

OUR neighbours to the left, the Stahl's and us, were not on speaking terms. When we passed their house we pretended they didn't exist. When I wandered through the back gate and sat in the orchard I imagined two property lines, which seemed the issue of the dissension: One drawn by them, the other by us and the disputed no-man's land in-between. East of Eden, with the fiery sword rotating, instead of exchanging fruit and vegetables across the fence, as I knew it had once been; where I sat under the trees dreaming it would one day be so again.

Then after we were expelled from our homes as landless refugees without property lines we heard that the Stahl's had likewise found shelter in a village nearby. I said to Mother, "Let's go for a visit," but she wouldn't hear of it.

Yet I kept persisting until she finally relented to my request. In the meantime, the Stahl family had also heard about us and we soon knocked on each other's doors, greeting each other like old friends. It was like the day of resurrection I had dreamed of while we exchanged presents – ours a cup of sugar, theirs a spool of thread, both rare treasures in those days, scrounged from our post-war rations.

Later as an adult, with fate having imposed the dual role of father and mother on me, felt like fate's betrayal and I again put a stop to my dreaming, depriving myself of its sweetness. If there are other dreamers out there, let me listen to their stories.

During my teenage transition I resented the fact that I was excluded from the cosmic council of decision-making. What kind of democracy is this? A franchise, as Jonathan said once. "I am a franchise of the cosmic corporation, and without a manual."

On the other hand, perhaps the manual is always close at hand. It's just that in my impatience I fail to consult its instructions, cultivating our chatter instead, until I forgot about its existence.

"The seed falling among the thorns refers to someone who hears the word but the worries of this life and the deceitfulness of wealth choke the word, making it unfruitful."

MATTHEW 13:22

When I am needy I take and take and what do I give in return? What in the end is reserved for God my Creator? How can He fit inside a space cramped with self-centredness? Should I send love letters to God, addressed to "Dearly Beloved?"

Dearly Beloved what?

Dearly Beloved, I apologize for the times I have failed to appreciate your gift called life – the gift from you to me.

Dearly Beloved, I thank you.

Thank Him for what?

Thank you for the privilege of being part of your creation, blessed with the opportunity to discover myself.

Sadly, in times of insecurity I have minimized and even tuned out what was provided, replaced with a tape itemizing what was missing instead with regrets of having failed to live up to my full potential, observing life through a lens of scarcity. I must confess how this insecure part frightens me when life becomes a scary responsibility, an unsteady ship I have to navigate while I pretend to have confidence in front of the other passengers. At intervals the sea rises to a gigantic mass when I doubt my navigational skills, transferring my nervousness. The journey that was to be a joyous adventure then becomes a struggle and some will jump overboard even though they can't swim. Others fail to comprehend the purpose of the journey but see it as a competition to hoard its gifts, depriving their fellow traveller of their share. But God doesn't give faulty gifts, does He? The surprise is that I don't have to accomplish anything other than being this gift to myself and arriving at my goal just the same. I still dream of a world free of borders and property lines. Once the old system proves to be unsustainable, I might be among the first lining up to support the change.

Amidst my North American material privilege, I pray for those who don't have this opportunity and

I pray for us to share it unilaterally with others – not through enforced revolution but according to the law of distribution.

So let me start all over again.

Thank you God for me, this gift from you that I don't always appreciate. Are you smiling?

PART III

Messages from the Periphery

Jonathan

CREATION

"HOW would creation define itself?" I ask my Maker.

Creation: I am the destroyer and the creator, as you are the destroyer and the creator in motion. I am all the components that you are part of. At times, the cycles make no sense to you and you lose faith and form your own doctrines, setting the stage for doubt to sneak in. It's when you wander out of orbit that you feel alone. Be reminded that the universe always provides the means to guide you back to safety but you must allow yourself to be guided.

"So what is the purpose of spinning through this orbit?"

"Life."

"What is the purpose of life?"

"The gift of life is life itself through which to express yourself and with the universe expressing itself through you."

"Okay, one more question. Where does the devil fit into this picture?"

"Why not direct the question to the source?"

CONVERSATION WITH THE DEVIL

"I am part of the orbit."

"How?"

"I am the mischief-maker."

"You mean you have permission?"

I repeat … I am part of the orbit, as you are part of it. I am the tester, the jester, the trickster who sprinkles titbits of temptations along your path to expose your personality. I am the stage director of the plays, the costume designer and the choreographer. Together you and I write the plays. What would an existence be without drama and a sense of play? The problem, or what you perceive as the problem, arises when you become addicted to the plays and you don't want to leave the stage, restricting yourself to your limited script. Then of course I get the blame once the play fails to make sense and you become frightened and say, "The devil made me do it."

Jonathan

A TRAVELLER ONCE EQUIPPED WITH WINGS

WHERE do I fit in among this cosmic drama, I ask.

The answer: You are a traveler once equipped with wings you have allowed to atrophy. A winged creature must remain attuned to the law of its spheres. When it gorges indiscriminately it will become bloated and sluggish and gravitate to the ground, polluting the environment.

How can I get my wings back?

You have to retreat into your silence and go on a mental, as well as a physical fast if you want to soar again and save your environment. Interesting, I say to myself. So, I have become one of many sedentary creatures too bloated to fly, foraging and polluting the Earth, and I suspect the polluting cannot be tolerated forever?

Not if you are unwilling to fast.

Who will pay the consequences?

It is Earth of course who will have to rid itself of the blight in order to save itself if the foraging and polluting birds with atrophied wings like me, are unwilling to fast. And I know the silence is the confirmation.

Next, my little voice awakens to reconfirm, "I tell you this, the best room is the quiet room within. Once you trust in the power of your own knowing and you cultivate this room with good intentions towards yourself and others, you will not have to run and seek for another to succumb what is counter-productive to your journey."

Leni

THE PERFECT PORTRAIT

I am life. Life proceeds to move on, regardless of the stragglers that fall behind. Life feeds on life. Even as I fade towards my final days and have barely anything to contribute any longer, will suck on the last spark of energy clinging on. Then in the end, what is left, other than the memories crammed in between – now gone as well? The illusions are gone, together with the dreams and the theories that kept my intellect alive. Perhaps these concepts don't want to die, but greedily try to latch onto the next generation. And what about the illusory soul I can neither touch nor photograph to frame for my children?

If, as Jonathan says, he is merely a franchise of this cosmic corporation, can this franchise attain independence or is it bound by contracts, in which case I would prefer the position of an employee not bound by contracts. Instead of a corporation liable to the corporation, I would rather pick daffodils and be free to move on at the end of the season.

Yesterday as I passed a church, people streamed from the open door, laughing and calling out to each other. Another wedding is sanctioned. The groom dressed in his elegant suit, the bride a creation of loveliness radiating like the dawn of creation, stepping out of the door ducking the pelted rice, running towards the limousine marked "just married" on their way to experience each other through each other. My poetic sentimentality takes over. I imagine what if, as in a fairy tale, this exhilarating moment were encapsulated in infinity. I imagine she is me and I utter the words: "May this moment last forever!" The cosmic camera snaps and we are dancing in perfect rhythm like a couple on top of a music box.

Then after a time experiencing this uninterrupted moment of perfection, an odd phenomenon stirs and I feel restless. I cry for movement to dance with my beloved outside this cycle. Even if his steps don't match mine I call for the experience to dance in the turbulence of life. I am awed by the experience even though its movements at times veer out of balance. Or I burst into tears overwhelmed by the gigantic waves that crash over me, making me gasp but reminding me that it is I who called for this partnership.

What about those who are excluded from this interacting experience? I must remind myself that time does not stand still, but churns out infinite opportunities regardless of its confinement to little calendar squares. I am the food I feed on – the consumer and the supplier. I am my own conspiracy theory, my power plant, my own corporation not bound by contract.

Jonathan

"CAN you explain the history of the Great Pyramid? "I ask my Maker.

The answer appears in visual form. A fierce storm is racing over the plains chasing dark clouds. After the clouds disperse, light beams flash across the sky, revealing a descending airship.

Once stabilized on firm ground, a door slides open. Tall figures wearing dark suits with light-grey trim step out and brace themselves against the clutches of the wind. They have travelled far, I am given to understand, and this is the site where they were instructed to build, in alignment with their home star. It is a design to serve as a purification system to drift like whiffs of incense across the planet and stabilize the turbulence that is raging out of control. Their own inherent vibrations are to serve as levers in the construction and as transformers to energize the chambers within the structure.

For their mission to succeed they must remain in balance with their personal integrity inherent in their truth. The IAMTHATIAM in tune with the final IAM. The trinity of the alchemist, the architect and the physicist direct the team.

But gradually, a sense of superiority showed its greedy head and disrupted the harmony of the team. The alchemist claimed personal credit for a job well done; the architect's ego burst with pride; the physicist expressed his lofty opinion.

The energy inside the pyramid didn't fail instantly however, as a number of the team still maintained their integrity.

Yet, eventually even amongst them, the majority succumbed to ambition, greed and power. They became the magicians of their time – some good and some evil-minded in their selfish desires.

Leni

I finally approach the subject that has been on my mind all along, asking the question with my note pad in hand.

SCHIZOPHRENIA

Imagine a variety of cosmic seeds, each containing the blueprint of its impending experiences. Some carry the predisposition to travel an alternate path to experience the lesson of fragmentation. It is a path where no directions have been mapped.

Observing this state of fragmentation in one you love requires moments of calmness. Take care not to contribute additional anxiety to an already stressed situation, lest the connection snap like an overstretched elastic and emotions jump in a choreography of distorted movements. You who are involved are anxious. This is understandable; you want a cure, and you want it now. Trust his/her path and you will bear no grudges towards fate and the world. This personality has a tendency to wander off, lured into mysterious other places. Its spirit must be allowed to explore these possibilities, with an intuition of what s/he came to learn. They do not force you into their experience so don't force yours onto them. Allow these individuals to draw their own plan and present their own case instead of measuring the chemicals so anxiously you might forget it's soul.

Trust their path, have compassion, and you will be rewarded with amazing discoveries, and feel uplifted by the lesson of generosity.

A PAST REVELATION

IT was after Mother's funeral that a former acquaintance of hers, Frau Schloesser, appeared from Germany and we sat up late talking. From her, I learned the story related to the accident earlier alluded to by Ivanka. Yes, I did have a brother once, his name was Matias and when one day Tati came back from riding and before Oma noticed, the child ran outside waving his little arms and said, "Look daddy, I have a 'tick'." He tapped the horse's ankle and the horse shied and kicked out, killing my four-year-old brother before I was born. Mother was away visiting Drago and Bianca. From that time on, mother shut herself in her darkened room, my visitor said, trying to digest the little food that she had forced down her throat. The priest during confession convinced her that her child's death was her punishment for her selfishness of having been a neglectful mother and by visiting people who danced the devil-invoked Scharleston.

This was the first part of the story.

The second part was that at the time of the accident Mother was in her third month of pregnancy with me. Having already suffered through two stillbirths prior to "the accident," she was convinced that this child she now carried in her womb was also destined to die. The moment I arrived, I cried and refused to eat. And mother's apparently already fragile nerves were unable to cope with this scrawny creature destined to die.

Oma's words about the curse echoed back, and the mention of the "cross" we had to bear.

I sat down and grieved for this family locked in their emotions that did their best to raise me. I cried because I loved them so and I grieved for all the baggage we had passed on to each other.

My visitor confirmed something else I had already suspected. Ivanka had become an underground informer for the Partisans.

We had a spy living in our house.

WAR CHILD CONTINUED

It could be your father, your brother, or sister –
it could be you

MY early school years are a recollection of political roller coasters smashing into each other. My first teacher was German. A Serb, arriving with his own baggage of indoctrinations, then replaced him. He hung a picture of the Czar above the blackboard looking disapprovingly down at us ethnic German children occupying the desks.

Having been raised in a German community, some of us were far from fluent in the Croatian language, let alone with Serb expressions. He would get furious and throw the soppy sponges used for wiping the blackboard, at us. Or order one of us to extend an open palm to receive the force of the willow switch. The primary humiliation was to expose a boy's buttocks in front of the class while the raised switch made whooshing sounds with each blow to the bare skin, and welts the thickness of ropes swelled up and I could read the silent fury on the boy's face.

The following semester, the German teacher was back, removing the picture of the Czar and replacing it with the piercing eyes of the Fuehrer. The Fuehrer liked his pictures taken surrounded by children with Aryan features – handsome boys and pretty girls with flaxen braids and sparkling-blue eyes like Anna's. There were photos of Aryan athletes with bodies like Greek sculptures. The Fuehrer didn't pose next to them and just as well because in comparison he couldn't live up to their Aryan image.

Then Tito came to full power, the fate of the ethnic German children took the same direction as Sara Rosenberg's, whose family had disappeared one day. Sara had the same peachy skin and blond hair as Anna's, although she was Jewish. There were rumours that were too scary to think about. One day the windows of their house were staring from a hollow emptiness and their store was plundered. Ivanka came home with a soft leather purse with a pretty clasp. Oma asked where it came from. From the Rosenberg house, Ivanka said. And Oma said, "It's not right to take things from another house, even if they aren't there for now."

"They were too rich," Ivanka said, "and they always looked down on me with their nose sticking in the air." It was just what I heard her say to Janos the stable hand one day about us: "They are too rich," although we didn't consider ourselves rich.

There were other parts that were not the same as they used to be. During fruit picking time, the gypsies – who used to this job, had also disappeared – about the same time as the Jewish people. I loved to watch the gypsies in their colourful clothing; and the sparks in the men's eyes as they followed the women's swaying hips that made their skirts sashay, and the way they tossed their hair. With the men, it was a language of the brows. The same as Janos used to behave in the presence of the girls who worked in the fields, making them giggle and refer to him as "that fiery Hungarian."

Too many changes took place too rapidly. It was no longer safe to drive through the countryside. Along the roads, limp bodies with twisted faces and swollen tongues dangled from telegraph wires. The last time we drove to Berak our hearts sank at the sight of the recent devastation and beside the road the gruesome sight of a dead Ustasha soldier with the symbol of the Croatian flag engraved into the skin on his back, lying beside the road. We turned around and headed back home.

Nervous eyes peeked from behind curtains and looting took place. Fear stuck to everything, it was a fear of the unpredictable. The next strung-up body could be a member of one's own family. While I pictured the angels shedding streams of tears, asking for someone to intervene, God seemed to have moved far away. Jesus had said all he had to say; his followers turned deaf. The crops that were to feed families demolished by air power and mechanical monsters, and disrespectfully trampled by boots too numb to recognize the sacredness of creation.

Jonathan

TOURISTS are taking a break in the square around the fountain, throwing chunks of left-overs to the pigeons where Saul-Paul used to come and soak up the sun. I sent a mental message for him to meet me.

At some point, it was clear that the message hadn't been received.

I hailed a taxi and asked the driver to circle the lower part of town with the drunken buildings leaning over. Each time I saw someone resembling Saul-Paul I stuck my head out to take a closer look. A couple of guys yelled obscenities.

"What exactly are you looking for, buddy?" the driver asked.

Suddenly the car swerved and stopped.

"What are you doing?" I asked.

He jumped out and asked for the fare with the door held open on my side.

I didn't want to argue but handed him the money, then hailed another cab; this time I asked to be dropped off along the bank. "Wait a minute," the new driver said, after I described Saul-Paul. "I read an article in the paper about a guy like him. Found under the apple tree near the bridge, it said – dead."

"Dead?"

"Yeah."

"But he said he was protected."

"Apparently not that day."

I walked to the nearby second-hand store where I found a statue of Jesus, then stopped at a flower shop, and last at a bakery where I picked up a croissant. Saul-Paul used to be fond of croissants. Next, I walked down to the apple tree where I shredded the croissant and tossed the pieces down the bank.

Crows swooped down, calling to each other and pecking at the pieces; a couple of gulls swooped to investigate and the crows took to the air.

"Poor broken bird," I said as I placed the potted plant under the tree next to the statue of Jesus.

Leni

A CONSTANT COMPANION

MY poor car is stranded beside the highway, its face bashed in with one eye bulging, the other torn from its socket. We are waiting for the police to arrive. I am hot and uncomfortable, while the next minute I am cold and shivering. Shards of glass are scattered over the road, crushed into pieces of crystal; a stream of oil oozes from its bowels. My eyes settle on the skid marks snaking across the road. I am fascinated by these marks that at the moment represent the vulnerability of my existence. I stand in awe of this fragility that is my strength. At the flip of a wheel, it can transport me from this dimension to another. These two realities are constant companions driving side by side. If I am curious about life, I am also curious about death.

Since we are so closely interconnected, why not get to know each other so that when my time is up, I can entrust him to fold me in his mantle and transport me to my place of rest.

"Hello, Death," I say, engaging him in dialogue as my car clunks along on the way to the nearest service station pulled by a tow truck. I sense he is a friendly fellow, free of cares, for Death has nothing to fear. It is I who wears the shirt of gloominess. Unformulated thoughts stir and tumble through my head, searching for coherence to spring forth as a question.

"It's not you I fear," I say. "In fact, I have welcomed you at times – it's the pain I associate with you that I fear."

"For those whose conscience is clear, there is nothing to fear," he tells me.

"How do I clear my conscience?"

"By helping others."

Jonathan

AFTER several weeks, the familiar voice is ringing through my head.

"Hello Earthling."

"Itak! Where did you disappear to?"

"I met a fellow Idrisian."

"Where is he staying?"

"His name is Ahsim, and he is keeping a low profile as your saying goes, and as according to my experience, I know that it takes time to adjust to your environment. When next we meet, I will tell you his story."

Ahsim's Story

AHSIM'S ship was hijacked by the ruling class of Planet S'yh, whose primary concern was to fuel their space ships to transport them to their secret colony, with the intention of leaving the starving population behind. It came to their attention that Ahsim's ship carried the technology to replenish the resources that were in scarce supply. But S'yh was not on Ahsim's list of replenishment.

Under prolonged days of torture, he weakened and revived a portion on their list they had depleted. With his request to be shared with the population. A request, they promptly ignored and proceeded to exploit. When Ahsim saw the results of their deception, and the abhorrent condition of its population, he chose mutilation over selling his integrity.

"How did he land on our planet?" I asked. But by now, only a strange buzz came through.

Leni

IF WHOLENESS MEANS CRAZINESS, THEN LET ME ESCAPE INTO IT

THERE is a place of wholeness, where I can cuddle myself and fall in love with myself. In this state of wholeness, lies the encyclopaedia of my knowing, where the restlessness of competition is laid to rest and judgement has no place to hide.

I believe there is a state of wholeness in each of us even in those who don't believe there is or who are afraid to expose their vulnerability, where all parts are breathing in synchronicity enjoying the partnership. Where I can trust to switch to automatic pilot.

Others will laugh at this idea. "Crazy, insane," they might say. But I picture a time when infinite numbers of us will recklessly run through the streets with awakening sparks of craziness, inviting each other to share the treasures they have collected.

"My cellar is stacked with vintage wines. Drop by for a taste."

"Come by to enjoy my garden if it gives you pleasure. Be sure to bring the kids!"

KATHARINA NOLLA

"The cottage hasn't been used for a while. Pick up the keys and invite your friends."

"I invite you over to relax by my fountain, to refresh your spirit."

"Now what is this, you sleeping on the street? Pick up your bag and follow me. You can use the spare room."

"Dad, how do soldiers killing each other solve the world's problems?"

BILL WATTERSON,
Calvin and Hobbes: Sunday Pages 1985-1995

I imagine this craziness to extend to the battlefields where suddenly all soldiers globally from all fronts decide on a "smoking break." Even those who don't smoke join in. They soak in the silence and gradually begin to look around and see their own weariness reflected in the eyes of their opponents. Here and there one of them dares to cross the demarcation line and share a cigarette from his/her pack, which leads to little gestures where the spoken language isn't understood. Soon one or another pulls a picture of loved ones from his/her pocket, while their neighbour shares his own. They look and nod with admiration at the little faces smiling back, a spouse, their parents, and tears well up in their eyes.

Gradually others cross the line, and then some more. Those who are bilingual engage in conversations. "I don't know about you, brother, but as for me, I am getting tired of this, you know."

They wearily stare at the ground, and take another puff. "You saw the little fellow in the picture. You know what he wrote in his last letter? It said, 'They say you are doing a good job out there, Dad. I hope you are doing a lot of shooting to finish your job so you can come home soon. I miss you, Dad.' Now what do you think of that?"

With a weary voice his neighbour utters, "I don't want to deprive your little fellow of his father."

"I feel the same, brother. Nor do I want to be the cause of breaking your wife's heart." They reach out and embrace, sobbing on each other's shoulder.

There are young mother soldiers from all sides whose little ones are left behind, exchanging stories. They who have given life now feel deeply ashamed for taking part in dishonouring the sacredness of life. Right then, these mothers make a pact that they will no longer take part in such a system.

Just as they become acquainted, the PA system goes wild, with both sides calling their soldiers back to duty.

An odd phenomenon occurs. No one moves.

The generals get involved, appealing to family values.

"Where are your own families, then? Why don't you drop them off to finish the job if it's so important to you," the soldiers call, supported by a lot of hooting and clapping.

Helicopters buzz above, dropping off reinforcements of generals, gesticulating and blaming each other for the congestion, hollering at each other to get their troops moving, launching into fistfights here and there.

On the field the soldiers' eyes light up, they begin to cheer and place bets. "Now here is something to write home about," some shout. The fields reverberate with laughter. "Where is the media?" others call. "Somebody take some footage to send home, the only thing that's missing is a few truckloads of beer!"

The generals can't believe their eyes at the troops' disrespect. They shout, "Cowards, yellow bellies, get your ass back to work!"

But the soldiers are having too good a time and they just keep laughing while the generals can't believe their eyes. The years of training and war psychology had not prepared them for this.

Jonathan

HIS RETURN

I would like to think that Saul-Paul and his buddy Jesus are now united in a dream of heavenly simplicity.

I am standing outside a church with organ music drifting out the door, a sign says to enter.

I enter.

I am handed a brochure: Pastor Oracle welcomes you, it says. Bow and you shall receive his blessings.

I bow.

Oracle nods from the pulpit and sends his blessing, with a gesture. "I must tell you that at this very moment, brothers and sisters, He is preparing for his return," Oracle calls out.

The morning sun is streaming through the windows, a gentle breeze flows from the side door. Two ushers pass collection baskets, around. Another, stacks of scrolls, while Oracle dreamily watches from his pulpit, and the baskets fill with cash.

Pointing to his own scroll, he shouts, "Yes, just as it says here, Jesus lives in me! Display this scroll in your living room for all to see, stick it to your refrigerator, your garage door. JESUS LIVES IN ME!"

He closes his eyes and drifts into a meditative mode, followed by a period of silence.

Suddenly, a voice interrupts the silence, "I am here," it says.

Oracle's eyelids flip up, his pupils stare into space.

"I am the Christ."

The scroll drops from Oracle's hand. His famous smile shrinks to an awkward slit, the background music fades. From below in the pews, an army of eyes stare at him. He tugs at his tie and retrieves his smile.

"Perhaps our visitor will care to join us," he says, addressing the congregation, their eyes focused on their pastor. He asks them to join him in praying for their country's brave soldiers who are fighting in the area their visitor was born in, to import peace and democracy to that troubled region. Christ responds by addressing the urgency of disarmament and nurturing the traumatized children back to health, in restoring the environment.

"Excuse me Lord," Oracle interrupts, "I appreciate your concern, and of course we have our agenda about the environment. But there is also the economy to consider, and people need jobs. ...As for going ahead with a plan for disarmament, at this point, sounds like a premature idea, if you don't mind me saying so."

Having said that, he can feel a sensation of blissful energy tingling up his spine. It seems to come from the presence beside him. Reminding him of an afternoon picnic when he was ten, eating cherry pie while his big sister played the guitar.

But this is no time to get distracted. He bends to pick up the scroll lying at his feet.

"When you look around, you will understand the resistance from those who don't value life, where as our nation has remained true to your principles."

Christ looks at him with eyes filled with compassion that have seen the wonders of heaven and the torments of hell. Rustling sounds stir from the benches. As Oracle looks down to sort his thoughts, he notices Christ's scuffed shoes, comparable with his own well-stitched designer brand, hopelessly out of style.

"Such loyalty is commendable," Christ replies. "Let's go."

"Let's go? Let's go where, Lord?"

"We will proceed from city to city, from one country to the next. The hungry are waiting to be fed, the sick crying out, the oppressed need to be heard."

Oral's eyelids flutter like a pair of butterfly wings. Maybe if he ignores this situation, it will go away. "Surely Lord, we can't jeopardize the safety of our people and risk the security of the free world by running off like some cult. Such strategy needs the approval of the State Department. We have to consult the president.

In the pews, the congregation awaits Oracle's decision. This time his eyes come to rest on Christ's threadbare shirt. He has to think. Perhaps there's a way to humour him, maybe he could suggest a private conference before the nation sees Him on their screen. Or persuade him to consult their tailor. He is a bit on the thin side and needs his hair styled, but with a bit of a makeover, anything is possible.

"Lord, can we retire to discuss this privately?" Oracle beams his winning best, "Perhaps over a meal of fish and figs, a glass of wine, if I may suggest?"

"The armed forces are invited to participate in the distribution," Christ continues, "and as I understand, the cash flow set aside for your current presidential election will cover the costs."

"Of course we honour your principles, but you wouldn't believe what we are up against."

"Then follow your principles."

As Christ steps forward to lead the way, the congregation wait for Oracle's decision. With a smile that cracks like old gyp rock, clad in his tailored suit, silk shirt and hand-stitched shoes, he follows Christ in his faded shirt and bleached-out cords and worn sandals, while contacting the State Department before things get out of hand.

Christ continues.

The congregation follows.

This time it will not be a public spectacle, Christ knows, but an affair of secrecy. A silent tear rolls down his cheek as he weeps for the potential he offered to unlock, now once more delayed for hundreds of years.

Jonathan, continued

If there is to be peace, maybe it's the Devil who could accomplish what the Ten Commandments failed to enforce, Jonathan speculates. He imagines all opposing heads of states locked inside one large barrack-style building. Here everyone would be required to share a common washroom and a kitchen where the meals are communally prepared. It would include doing the laundry and folding the sheets in pairs in a 7 AM to 10 PM schedule and with no hired help allowed. No one would be allowed to leave until the art of negotiation was understood.

In my dream last night, I removed the top part of my cranium that serves as the lid to my brain, because it felt too stuffy inside and needed fresh air to flow through. This activity attracted little fairies to hover above.

Peering down, their hands made fanning gestures and pinched their noses. Exchanging meaningful looks, they fluttered away with giggling sounds trailing behind.

Do fairies see and smell what I fail to see and smell?

If my head is a poorly insulated vessel, who knows what else is trapped inside. Will someone invent a brain vacuum, please! There must be plenty of brains in need of a good cleaning job.

Leni

WAR CHILD

(It Has Glory Written Across it)

> *"What difference does it make to the
> dead, the orphans and the homeless,
> whether the mad destruction is wrought
> under the name
> of totalitarianism or in the holy
> name of liberty or democracy?"*
>
> **MAHATMA GANDHI**

A November wind is whipping the trees. It's Remembrance Day.

Each Remembrance Day I am drawn to watch as veterans stand erect in front of the cenotaph while saluting to the sound of a bugle. Some have medals pinned to their chest. It is as if I am looking on with the awareness of a child, trying to complete a puzzle.

What is the association to this puzzle I ask?

The answer appears in my dream. In this dream, night descends and calls forth a vision: I am standing in a field obscured by mist. A pale figure wrapped in a dark cape floats towards me. I know, it's death.

Identical cross-shaped stones line the field in even rows. I wonder how I have failed to notice before that I am standing in a graveyard.

I see that fresh mounds have popped up from the grounds. The mounds begin to stir. Replicas of men in uniforms as at the cenotaph rise in the air, asking me to show them the way home. Contrary to the veterans at the cenotaph, however, in my dream they are each wearing a Peltzkappe – the same as grandmother's cousin Toni used to wear, a cap made from Persian lamb.

Huddled in a corner, a little hunch-backed figure grins at me, all the while clutching a flag. Powder kegs of ammunition are exploding all around. I ask why everyone is shooting at people they don't even know. The little figure in the corner grins and raises its flag. It has the word "glory" written across in front and back.

The men in veterans' uniforms rising from their graves, are now asking,

"Why did we have to die?"

"How did you die?" I ask.

In the background bombs are raining down the answer. Everywhere I look, fingers are attached to triggers pulled in repetitious motion. A tank is being hit and scorched bodies pop from its hatch, transformed into grotesque sculptures, with stiff fingers pointing to the sky.

I ask what kind of existence is this and they say they don't know, but why did they have to die? Somewhere on the side, a child is watching, telling them, "You may go back to sleep."

When I woke up I knew that child, for she is me.

What was this dream trying to tell me, I asked when I woke up? What was the association of the veterans in the graveyard wearing replicas of cousin Toni's Peltzkappe?

March 1944

When Tati opened the newspaper one morning, his cousin Toni's face was splashed across the front page wearing his usual trademark Peltzkappe. The caption of the paper announced, "Local hero saved his town."

We had a celebrated hero in the family.

It said that Toni stormed into the night and single-handedly fired on a group of invading Partisans, that two were killed and the others ran away.

Later rumours circulated saying they might not have been Partisans but merely a group of prowlers.

The impact of this story impressed on me the realization that tomorrow a soldier from any side could perform a heroic act by shooting us, without knowing anything about us, and this was the association with Toni' s Peltzkappe in the dream.

Jonathan

THE MACHINE

I am watching an air show at the military base. Stream-lined planes take to the sky, glistening in the sun as they perform acrobatics while the onlookers cheer and clap.

Parked at the periphery of the field, I notice a heavy-bellied machine that no one seems to pay attention to. It looks sad.

I walk over and ask, "Why are you so sad?"

It looks at me by opening the shutters of its machine eyes large and submissively "I am sad because I am sched-uled for another so-called assignment. I am sad, because during my assignments I am made to roar and pound at targets below." At times I feel as if am possessed by evil spirits making it their headquarters." Wailing sounds have drifted from below and it wonders if perhaps living creatures are involved in the pounding. This suspicion is clearly tormenting its machine mind, compounding its depression.

I want to help this big machine that has to roar and pound at dubious targets when it longs to be gentle, and I know it wants me to take charge because it feels so small. And we feel sad together.

"If I had the skill, I could de-program your schedule and cancel the orders of the assignment," I say. "But I have the feeling that this wouldn't be the right decision. Because the other side would as promptly re-program you. Think how this would affect your nervous system. No, we have to consider this carefully."

"I wish I could hide, you," I say, "but you are too big."

"There might be another way," it says. "At times they launch into fierce arguments. Maybe if I added to their annoyance, they might fight each other and forget about me."

"No," I protest, "stirring up additional dissension is not the answer."

So I console it with the assurance that the day will come when there will be no more destructive assignments, but all of its kind will be occupied by happy spirits.

"When?" It anxiously wants to know.

But I cannot give a date. All I can give is hope.

Leni

AT THE EDGE

(War Child)

IT was during summer 1944 after Tati's death, when mother and grandmother were conversing in low voices. It had to do with some papers that Tati had left behind and were to ensure our safety in case we had to escape. These papers had to be delivered to a certain address. They tried to think who could be entrusted with this mission then decided there was no such person.

"I will go," I said.

They looked at me and then looked at each other. It had to be secretly done at night and the streets were no longer safe and there were too many spying eyes, they said.

After further deliberation, I slipped out into the night with the paper pinned to the inside of my slip.

The streets and sidewalks were deserted, the walls of the familiar houses loomed like alien fortresses, where bodies could jump from doorways, with the curtains tightly drawn across the windows. I was headed for the house where the White Russian lived who had escaped the Bolsheviks. He was a notary by trade.

Raids – from all sides, were conducted at night. Throats were slashed and people dragged away, never to return. It was during that walk that I created a mental mechanism that to this day remains useful. I have applied to my travels when I found myself in dubious situations. I willed myself to dissolve into a state of invisibility.

When I arrived at the designated house, I threw a ball of wool at the upstairs window, as instructed. A slight movement stirred the curtains and shortly the door opened that led into the courtyard. I had seen this man on his walks swinging his ornate cane. That was when strangers still greeted each other and nationalities were not considered an issue. Upstairs, the windows were covered with black sheets underneath the white lace curtains. He wordlessly extended his hand.

After I turned and unpinned the envelope from my slip, he sat down and through a magnifying glass scrutinized the pages, while chewing on his lower lip, which made his goatee quiver as he carefully obliterated some dots and letters. Some that he replaced with others.

When the job seemed complete, he frowned and stroked his goatee, then pulled out a handkerchief to wipe the moisture from his forehead.

"Remember not to tell anyone that you were here," he said before I walked out with the envelope pined back to my slip. I would have liked to ask questions concerning the papers but he was already ushering me towards the door.

Back in the dark street, the dogs began to bark and I knew it was a sign to make myself invisible. It was always the dogs that warned us, heralding the ominous pounding boots, making us tremble. When I arrived back home, mother and grandmother were waiting in their own darkened room. Mother looked at me and said, "If father were here he would be proud of you." It was the only time I remembered my mother showering me with praise and I felt proud and strong. This experience shaped my attraction for adventure, at times testing life at the edge.

THE EDGE

ADJACENT to the mining camp up on the north shore of Lake Athabasca, I was introduced to Joe and Rita, a native couple, whom Pau had befriended and who still lived the traditional way.

On Pau's days off, he would borrow their frisky team of huskies tied to their sleigh, and with me serving as ballast, feeling like an immortalized ice maiden, we raced across the vast stretch of frozen lake with the temperature close to sixty below.

Later in our courtship, in mid-summer after the ice had melted, we took three weeks off, rented Joe and Rita's old canoe with its antiquated outboard motor and prepared for a trip into the unmapped wilderness. The news travelled and when it reached R.C.M.P. headquarters, they paid us a visit to warn us that a rescue mission would be out of the question in this vast territory.

Undeterred by the warning, we chugged away, I with my toes and fingernails painted a deep red and my underwear I had ordered from Fredericks of Hollywood packed into the duffel bag along with my designer bikini I had bought on a trip to Montreal.

In the second week the clouds turned angry, the waves surprised us with their ferocity; the rain began to pelt down and the canoe sprang a leak. My job was to bail out the water with an empty tin can while Pau remained pre-occupied with the navigation and with appeasing the sputtering motor. Only once, as I glanced at the gigantic granite walls lining the shore, did it briefly occur to me that should the waves hurl the canoe against this formidable barricade its hull would shatter and we might become immortalized in the R.C.M.P.'s records, with our bodies never to be retrieved or formally buried. Then I pushed the thought aside and continued to dip the can where the water seeped through. The next day the sun was shining and we crossed another stretch of rapids with the canoe on Pau's strong back.

Being an area uninhabited by humans, a bear would appear along the shore now and then, looking at us while we stopped to build a fire to cook the fish we caught that were still plentiful before the uranium tailings were dumped into the lake. At intervals we removed the black flies that had found their way in between the socks and the tied-down jeans, creating black anklets. While the following day we would each resume our assigned roles with Pau the navigator at the helm of the canoe and I his mate with the tin can close at hand, exploring another stretch of territory.

CONNECTING WITH MY EMOTIONS

AT times life sails through uneventful stretches of territory, giving me a break from its complexities and from myself. At other times, it churns and heaves and spits out emotions that make me gasp.

If I interviewed these emotions how would they interpret their role?

FEAR'S INTRODUCION: You portray the Devil with horns attached to his head, which is really a misplaced portrait of me. It's when you shut me away within your prison of denial that you perceive me as a scary distortion, and miss the lesson I am to teach you.

I am the catalyst that prompts your insecurities out of hiding. My job is to push you to the edge of panic to gulp for air, forcing you to breathe beyond your shallowness. At which point I become your ally in removing obstacles out of the way even while you shake and quiver in the process. In some ways, I am like a bird that feeds on parasites to clean your environment. See my job as a rehearsal to your self-reliance, rewarded on the stage of life.

EMOTIONAL SUFFERING: I express myself in varying degrees of intensity to test your endurance, and while you gasp and struggle, you at times see me as a curse that conspires against you. The resistance, the excuses and justifications that surface are incredible when alternate methods are suggested. Or you check out altogether missing out on the solution that tried to point out what doesn't work, depriving yourself of its valuable lesson.

Examine your diagnosis closely. The negativity attributed to me might just be a stormy day that doesn't last forever; and through the crack of darkness is the certitude of light, the catalyst of transformation.

ANGER: Imagine a sea crowded with countless anchors. Instead of contributing to a sense of stability, these anchors are designed to operate in a constant state of agitation. Even those attempting to stabilize have difficulty retaining their equanimity.

As the principal anchor, it is my task to assist the little anchors churn up the debris of emotions that has settled at the bottom of your sea.

In the process of keeping this technology running, I have to focus on my own survival that operates at the edge of destruction that at any moment can blow itself up like a suicide bomber. I tell you, there are times when I am so depleted, not knowing how much longer I can last at this job. Look up Atlas on the web and you will understand my task, which is as colossal as trying to hold the globe on his shoulders. These Greeks certainly did have a knack for drama.

Therefore, don't add me to the list of your enemies, but allow me to steer you towards alternate practices in stabilizing your affairs. Compare the process to the irritation to a grain of sand in the oyster, producing a pearl.

ENVY: I am laughing, because among the list of emotions I have hit the jackpot. I am your pet indulgence, your well-kept secret, and when no one is around and looking, you invite me in, indulging me with titbits of gossip and I purr like a pampered kitten as you entertain me with your list of stories and your ingredients of justifications.

I tell you, we all have our instinct for survival and I just continue to slide into the spot that feeds me, finding my way even through the tiniest crack, and in some places the door remains wide open. I am another by-product of failed aspirations you don't want to acknowledge – your unrequited desires, your unfulfilled dreams. You have your monasteries and various spiritual centres that claim to keep me out but even there, although slightly diluted, I find refuge in its hierarchy to claim a time-share on the Real Estate of its altar, enjoying a good time.

JOY: I relish being of service, dancing to draw your attention and brighten your spirit. I wave from each blade of grass. I announce myself through the rustling of the leaves and the sunbeams I glide on. The laughter in the eyes of children, the moon's admiration reflected on the water, the cooing of a baby.

I encourage the legs of the runner, infuse the steps of the dancer, and caress the strings of guitars.

I arrive at the scene of death, stroking the brow of the departing, reflected in the eyes of compassion. I will not give up on my role, but whisper encouragement even to those who were raised on a mantra that life is a struggle.

I keep dancing, dancing, because I am joy and will not allow myself to be affected otherwise no matter what viruses might hang around.

I can be found in the sound of the waterfall, the twirling of a snowflake, the bonding between mother and child and father. I am found in the embrace of lovers, in the flight of birds, and in dreaming the dream of creation.

LOVE: I thank you for your invitation. It's this invitation that contributes to my energy. But be reminded not to lock me into false relationships of co-dependence or treat me as an exclusive possession. Enjoy the spark, no matter how brief. Emotions come in waves and it is you who has control of their flow. During the years of marriage, some of you become disappointed with the relationship and this becomes a great challenge, like keeping a flame alive during a storm. Don't waste the opportunity of my involvement and don't be frightened of my overwhelming passion.

Just as I am sorting out the last chapters to type into my journal, a scruffy-looking character appears at my mind door, demanding an interview.

It's impossible to define its gender under the filthy rags.

"No more interviews," I say. "The office is now closed."

It continues to glare at me; the smell is unbearable. I might as well get this over with.

"All right, but it has to be brief ... by the way, who are you?"

"Ho, ho, ho, centre stage political incorrectness. I will tell you who I am. My name is Hate. And I really don't give a shit who wants to stick to their denial of my association. Some will even pretend that my clothes are clean and my smell sweet as long as they can implicate me to their advantage.

"You like to deny me from the vocabulary of your homeland, but will cleverly export me into the territory of others like an injection of smallpox.

I make no distinction where I am dropped off, but unquestionably go about my assignment. If the job is to instigate a regime change to weaken the foundation of the neighbourhood or take sole charge of the resources, I will be there to lend my expertise to stir the dissension. My eyes feast on the sight of flesh stuck to the doorposts from the aftermath of battle, where the cooking pots still show evidence of life that had once flourished.

"But you know what? We all have our little secrets and once you no longer support and refuse to feed me, I will be willing to negotiate for alternate entertainment."

Roaring with laughter, it walks into the approaching night, I get up and close the door and burn sticks of incense to diffuse the stench.

"If we miss this opportunity, it may be a long time before we have another."

TIBETAN BOOK OF THE DEAD

A woman was in a coma. Suddenly she had a feeling to be at the gates of heaven. She heard a voice asking her:

Who are you?

"I am the wife of the mayor."

"I didn't ask you whose wife you are. But who are you?" The voice asked again.

"I am the mother of four children."

"I didn't ask you whose mother you are but who are you?"

"I am a teacher," the woman tried again to answer the question.

"I didn't ask you for your profession…"

And so it went on. Finally, as she couldn't answer that question

She was sent back to earth to find out who she really was.

WHO AM I?

I am a human being like my counterparts sharing this space. I am an assortment of electrons, protons, neurons, dendrites and chromosomes. I am complex chemicals, where the churning never stops. My journey leads through landscapes of fogged-in days and fierce winter storms, and overcast skies that eventually clear and let the sun shine through. I am a collection of stories that are to explain who I am.

Am I fallible?

As a human, I struggle with certain addictions and habits I cling to. At times, it seems simpler to hand my affairs over to a master a so-called guru; or to buy into a corporate system that promises protection with a comfortable lifestyle wrapped in the package. Then as long as I am allowed to mutter and complain a bit and have access to a variety of products provided by the market and a comfortable amount of credit to do the spending, I can convince myself that I have bought into a sane corporation that allows me my little indulgences.

How to be or not to be are questions debated by the philosophers, interpreted by preachers who claim to have the answers and by governments that take non-active actions.

My reactions will influence my actions and that in the end is all that I am responsible for.

The mystery continues, this me, this Human, the perpetual source of exploration.

'How did I get here?' 'Where did I come from?' Children ask these questions, addressed to the adults. Adults, having left childhood behind long ago, few remember.

Leni

WHAT AM I DOING HERE?

(The Cry for Freedom)

> *There's a luggage limit for every*
> *passenger on a flight. The same rules*
> *apply to your life. You must eliminate*
> *some of the baggage before you can fly.*
>
> **ROSALIND JOHNSON**

MY answer comes in the form of my own innate advice:

When you park in front of a stop sign, don't forget to move. If the direction is unclear, don't wail, "Who can I trust to show me the way?" Signal that you are in charge, instead.

I recall a period during my younger years when my friends and I searched for the answers in ancient scriptures and predictions, believing their information had greater credibility than ours. But the time has come to trust in my own knowing.

Meanings: Regardless of the meanings I attach to my reactions, they remain but meanings. But once I associate them with their source, I can liberate myself of their dependence.

Having been raised under various states of total-itarianism, the cry for freedom is never far away. This word evokes an image of me standing ankle deep in muck, however. How does the concept of muck associate with freedom, I ask? Then I understand that as long as I continue to mutter and complain, this means that some unresolved issues are hidden away, and nothing will change as long as my mindset doesn't shift. At times I have judged people as complacent when they failed to react as I thought they should at the news of innocent people being blown up, hiding in their little corner of denial as if this were hap-pening on another planet.

Yesterday I joined a peace march winding through the streets. The sight of the waving placards invariably triggers a feeling of anxiety in me. I understand that the placards are to make a statement, but my memories asso-ciate placards with enforced slogans and marching boots pounding the pavements, indicating another invasion.

When we arrived at our destination in the square, a young man looking like a dashing revolutionary in a movie claimed the stage to make his own statement, with some name-calling woven into his speech, which made me uncomfortable. My memory cried out, "Be careful! Don't adopt the same tactics that you came to protest against."

When later we met and sat by the fountain, I com-mended him for his passion and then explained a bit of my own reaction based on my early history while he shared his bagel with the pigeons. When I toned down my reaction, admitting that he was doing his best, the image of standing in layers of muck became clear. It represents my accumu-lated frustration that, combined with the collective, can cover miles of like additional layers. If the muck gets too deep, instead of insisting on my self-righteousness, I could consider engaging in some scrubbing, instead. The final gift I could then offer the world, is to drop my frustrations into the collective basket on the infinite altar of transformation, what seemed of such importance then would disintegrate, and this, spells freedom. Where I could finally contribute to the Christmas wish of "Good will on Earth, and peace to all mankind." And in the midst of my suffering my darkest hours can transcend as the brightest lessons, enhancing my evolution.

TO BE HUMAN

Is a series of breakdowns and renewal.

Of hopes and shattered dreams.

It is also about love! Bordering on the profane and the sacred.

The secret is that I get to the head of the race, not by striving, but awakening to surrender to life; bringing me a step closer to its embrace.

The final moment of awareness in search of myself, arises when I step out of myself, and I observe this person preoccupied, running to-and-from, looking worn and stressed and I recognize that this is me, trying so hard to make this work, and I am overcome with compassion. I know I can give permission to love and accept myself as I am. Again, and again reminding myself that I am my vehicle of transcendence. That life is also about laughter and sharing. Taking time out to be with myself.

Jonathan

I am watching the neighbour's cat stalk though the grass. They seem such secretive creatures, playful one moment, aloof the next; contrary to dogs that lick and slobber all over you and let their emotions hang out.

All is peaceful here and I drift off to sleep. When I wake up, the cat is still around, minding its business by sniffing the grass and marking its territory. "How are things in your world," I ask, "and how do you see us humans?"

All is fine, I am told, other than the days we arrive with our noisy machine the lawnmower, and traumatizing the poor little creatures nestling in the grass, making it their home. "Imagine yourself in their place," it says, "living in a world where a monster machine unpredictably arrives to demolish your home."

As for how you appear to me: "Let me tell you, there is no one who knows you better than your cat, and your cat is not impressed with your choice of lifestyle compulsively running around in "achieving" more than you already have, wearing yourself out to the point of exhaustion. That's when we cuddle next to you, trying to distract you from your overloaded intellect.

"Watch and learn, we communicate in cat language. Allow your body to express its wisdom."

You humans do, of course, control our lives and have done so since the idea of domestication entered your head. When you see us aloof and detached, give us credit for the enormity of our achievement. To have created a world of tranquillity within your chaotic drive.

Unfortunately, some of us having been raised in a negative environment, ugly scenes erupt at times when counselling is necessary and passive resistance is suggested.

"But to you who respect our rights by having formed THE SOCIETY FOR THE PREVENTION OF CRUELTY TO ANIMALS, to you, we express our gratitude"

Leni

FACT OR FICTION

*"To see your drama is to be liberated
from it."*

KEN KEYES

I imagine myself looking down at us through the mind of another-dimensional perspective: Observe us roaming through mazes called malls, with shelves and bins and carts stacked with food while at the same time in other parts of the globe, children with crusty eyes, bloated bellies and stick arms are dying of starvation as a result of empty shelves or no shelves at all. It is a world where commerce is driven by competition zooming through tunnels with one-way traffic where the survival rate is fierce and guaranteed to take its toll. Forward or die.

How would they make sense of what we categorize as wealth and poverty? Would they consider the ferocious hunger of the corporations as the poor consumed by a mentality that can never produce enough material results?

I imagine that one day I will look up and there, advertised in large letters, a sign says:

LIFE SCHOOL – ALL ANSWERS PROMPTLY DEFINED.

I step inside to study the brochures and to my surprise find the guidelines pretty straightforward. I empty my purse and reach for the sign-up fee.

But weeks later, inundated with information matched with the right answers, and while looking at the other students reflecting my own pale skin and lustreless eyes devoid of passion, I decide to opt out and go back to my own desk to take over my neglected administration.

Jonathan

MOTHER and I are rustling through the woods looking for mushrooms. She enjoys this nature stuff, knowing where to look. She is prattling on about something but I am in a fog, searching through the fog. The odd word begins to slip through. "Foolishness," is one of them, and something about half of life being preoccupied about managing instead of living life.

Then it's something about blueberries in the Ontario woods and again I try to wade through the fog. Some remembering is emerging.

Memory: I am in the woods, I taste the blueberries and then see the bear show up, and mother tells me to be very still. The bear's nose is twitching, as if trying to figure something out, and mother's arms tightly encircle my waist. After a while the bear clearly lost interest in us and waddled away. We picked a few more blueberries and then walked to the car. Mother asked if I was scared and I said "a little." And she said its okay to be scared at times.

Now in the present, I turn to her. "I remember what happened in the woods when we stopped to pick blueberries."

"The bear?"

"Yes."

She looks pleased that I remembered and I regret not having introduced her to Itak. I think Itak would have enjoyed these walks with Mother.

Leni

MY PARTICIPATION IN THE SPIN

I give myself credit for my bravery of this challenging participation in this spin navigating the seas of the human emotions. I dream for us to one day evolve to a level of joining the galactic union that so far have dismissed us as unacceptable on account of our warring addiction and the destructive treatment of our environment, which imposes a negative effect on the overall cosmic creation.

I envision the time when messages are dispatched, conveying our willingness to co-operate in becoming responsible neighbours. Appointments are made, contracts signed, and I certainly wouldn't want to miss that opportunity.

I am rewarded with a vision: In that vision, a short pasty-looking creature as in a 1980's ad of the Pillsbury dough boy, with a trumpet in hand, is standing on amount. It radiates an air of sweetness, which I can only describe as a state of bliss.

As it raises the trumpet to its lips, I understand this is an announcement to celebrate my return to myself. The sound of the trumpet send shivers of ecstasy up my spine, relaying a message that every moment when one of us steps from despair back into the light, heaven rejoices, adding to the numbers of co-creators. When I woke up, my inner voice announced, "There is nothing a shift of consciousness can't resolve," and I understand that this was my spirit guide speaking. For the second time reassuring me that I am my own self-contained vessel from where I can give birth to myself. Reminding me to cultivate my quiet room with good intentions towards myself and others."

Jonathan

"LEEYULEEYULI, hello Earthling!"

"Itak! Leeyuleeyuli, where are you calling from?"

"Ahsim and I have arrived back home."

"Congratulations, any little Ahsim/Itak seedlings in the plan?"

"We have a saying here: Once your accounts have been settled and your debts fully paid, then you are no longer restricted by time and space. In our case, we were advised to postpone such a plan for now until we are fully cleared of the energy we were exposed to on our expedition.

"I have been given to understand my dear friend, that this has to be our last communication because of the tremendous amount of energy that is required, and not to be abused. The other news is that my request to return back has been granted, and Ahsim has decided to join me. We will return as teachers by awakening your memory as it once was in the garden of your previous existence, pure and joyous. Mothers shall feel loved and fathers understood, and children given the gift of unconditional acceptance."

At this point, sounds of interference crackled through the line, and then cleared again.

"Teachers will no longer be required to repeat formulas that are already obsolete, doctors will believe in the power of healing; religions unilaterally pray together."

"How did you get back?"

"We were picked up by an Idrisian rescue ship."

"How about those who weren't rescued?"

The crackling sounds interfered again. "They will have a chance to slide through the next portal shift. But now I must hurry and I say, Leeyuleeyuli, and as your saying goes, take care, dear friend."

I was just going to ask about the portal shift but all I could hear was another crackle and a faint, "I miss you."

"Leeyuleeyuli, I miss you too," but I don't know if she could hear me.

Yesterday on my way downtown, I passed the pond in the park. "Hello, duck friends," I said. "Do you remember my companion with the crackling red hair?"

Downtown, the crowds behaved as if the circus had come to town. It's election time. Everyone is rallying for the particular candidate they think will deliver their dream. Each candidate focuses on accusing the other side of working toward the ruin of the nation and pointing out the mess the last government has left behind, without having a specific plan of their own. Should cracks and leaks appear in the foundation, the patch-up crew is sent into the night while its citizens are asleep, hoping the job will hold for their present term, and let the next government deal with the collapse.

I connect with my Maker. "I have a suggestion," I offer. "Let those who thrive on competition in accumulating positions of power and piles of money have their fun, and those who prefer to be employees be employees. The difference is that at the end of the year all the profits and the resources are to be shared equally.

Leni

IT SLURPS AND SPITS

IT makes me tremble, at times seems to tear me apart. It exposes my ultimate vulnerability and voraciously sucks, slurps, and swallows and spits me out again.

It makes me cry and express my frustrations but also makes me laugh and inspires me to love.

It is an experience that, once embraced, is awe and wonder.

It's called life.

The biggest obstacles standing in the way of progress occur when I confine myself to my little corner of complacency and shut out its voices – including my own. Or occur when I demand that others are indebted to love me.

In the overall pattern every star, cloud, the wind, and the blades of grass, the trees and the rocks, the creatures of the sky, the land and sea, and I, myself, are a creation of like spirit.

But why does the journey at times have to be so difficult?

Could it perhaps be that my attitude has something to do with it?

I envision a day, as I had envisioned as a child, when I would see the world united, with our hearts connected and with nothing standing in each other's way to fulfil our vision.

At that moment, I who am unable to cry, will cry so hard that the floodgates of joy will open and great puddles will form at my feet.

Dream the dream of my beloved Creator – of a world without borders, as simple as the equation as 1+1=2.

The impossibilities made possible.

In a world without boundaries even the cynics will have to admit to the possibility of the dream and for civilization to thrive.

Outward energy drawn inward turns into matter, whereas the light I generate is my spirit moving outward, as the sun that cannot live in any light except in which it radiates.

Jonathan

CYCLES OF EVOLUTION

ACCORDING to my Maker, there were periods in evolution where our bodies differed in shape and form from our current, and various legends attest to these times. One of these legends referred to the Zemelites whose lifestyle required no hands in the shape of our current. Nor, did they cover their bodies with garments. They paid homage to a serpent they revered for its cleverness.

One day this serpent projected to the Zemelites images on how the Gods lived and convinced them that they were entitled to a similar lifestyle. This revelation made a great impression on its audience who sent a petition to the source, encouraged by the serpent.

"What you were shown is an illusion," Creator God replied, "paid actors on a stage. Look at me. Am I bedecked in plumes and jewels as you were shown? Clad in silk and velvet as depicted, to impress each other? Do I live in a dwelling called a palace? Why do you demand a mirage? I have given you refreshing springs to quench your thirst and bathe in, fragrant sanctuaries as resting places and the fruits of paradise.

I have given you the magnificent creature called peacock to feast your eyes, the butterfly, the swan and flamingo, and all that is compatible with your environment to grace your surroundings. Spring blossoms and summer flowers, dewdrops and the stars at night. I have given you the flowing rivers and the cascading waterfalls, the marshland with its chirping fowl. The snowflakes of winter, babies with silky skin."

But they insisted on the lifestyle they were shown, tempted by the serpent.

Creator God said, "If this is what you wish, I will bestow your request on you but you must assume responsibility for the consequences of your choice; this is my covenant."

They had decided, they said. And yes, they agreed to the covenant He demanded.

God gave them a suitable plot and all that was requested, and more. This period was called the first and the second day.

Years went by, and they seemed to have settled in.

But one day as He came to check up on things as God usually did, the entire tribe stood in front of Him, their eyes fixed in silent confrontation. They complained about the mechanism of the hands that in their opinion weren't efficient enough to accomplish what they had envisioned. They were prone to injuries and suffered from the cold, and their new bodies made them sweat, and they didn't like to sweat, they pointed out. God once more reminded them of their covenant, and that these were the bodies they had requested, as shown in the video.

At that, they turned and walked away with renewed determination to realize their dream of progress.

As time progessed, an inspiration clicked in one of the tribal brains, plotting a plan that prevented him from sweating in the process of his ambition by subjugating others to perform the work. He convinced these subjects that it was in their interest to serve, in exchange for protection, he promised to provide. This subjugated lot built the high structure that was called a palace. Artists were ordered to create sculptures of lions and eagles and the serpent became immortalized. Images of stars sparkled on the dome-shaped ceilings. Murals of waterfalls cascaded down the walls with flowers painted in brilliant colours. The subjugated numbers who didn't know they were subjugated, paused and looked up occasionally, awed by the splendour accredited to their superiors and passed on to their progeny, reclining in the shade sipping fragrant drinks served to them. New names were categorized to clarify the division between kings and the subjects who grew the food and fought the battles for those established in the palace.

The Third Day: The invention of machines.

Machines could do the job faster than hands, and rapidly gained in importance with the progeny of the kings now divided into nations, which competed with each other. The superiority of the nation was now categorized according to the destructive power of their machines.

But gradually great numbers of the subjects (now referred to as the population) found the machines intimidated them. They had become an unpredictable obsession, causing increasing damage and loss of life as the drive of warfare became an obsession. The population marched and protested, mothers feared for the lives of their babies. But how inconsequential were the lives of babies in comparison to the machines as viewed by the men and women standing on their Olympian Heights, behaving as though they had mastered the laws of God.

The leaders of the Nations became the priesthood administering to the machines. The population were ordered to pay tribute. Eventually, the population became confused and divided as they watched the machines destroy what they had laboured over. Some said they needed the machines at any cost. Others said no, not at any cost.

The high maintenance of these machines with their destructive power resulted in scarcity throughout the lands and untold homelessness. The justification from the Super Nation was that they had to stand on alert against other nations who produced too many machines, while they stockpiled their own in vast numbers. What they feared most were countries that produced too many machines. The competition depleted the fuel that was to heat the people's homes and sucked tremendous amounts of water from the reservoirs. Nevertheless, some still opted in their favour, claiming that the machines provided leisure time to do bigger and better things, and because they didn't like to go back to sweating.

When the machines demanded the high profits cashed in by its investors, even they woke from their slumber and were frightened at what they saw. Yet, when the cry for change reverberated through the lands, too many still faltered, and the great power of the machines ignited, devouring the protesters along with the loyalists and their bank accounts.

Leni

I regularly meet with a circle of friends for what we refer to as our "homework class." The purpose is to explore life from different angles. When we are in harmony, our spirits sing to each other. I am them and they are me.

When I sit on the deck of my cottage to gaze at the stars, I imagine them singing to each other. The child in me then wonders which of these were once my previous home.

One could point out that the stars are not always attuned but at times collide, which some of us perceive as destruction. But I like to imagine that the stars know better. It is their task to nudge each other lest they doze off into complacency, which would extinguish their spark. It is their task to intermittently climax into explosions to scatter their seed to distant spaces in a dance of co-creation, expressing their love for the universe.

So it is within our homework circle. To an outside observer our methods might seem to clash but like the stars, we know better and by agreement dare to nudge each other, thereby seeding fresh thought-forms into creation. Katie nudged Glenn today when he seemed to get stuck in a mood of complacency. In her love for him, Katie wants to inspire him to reach his peak potential, as he is designed to be.

Jonathan

HIGH-PITCHED sounds assault my ears. It's the whining of a chainsaw as metal teeth grin sadistically, sinking into its trunk of what must be the last tree in the area. The tree hits the ground in a state of shock at the indignity of its execution. I shudder at the horrifying thought of searing tar soon be poured over another patch of precious earth skin in preparation for an additional parking lot. How can anyone derive joy from stretches of concrete? It has no sense of playfulness but spreads in dense indifference, where all pride has fled. All it knows is to be trod and pounded on by the invasion of rubber tires.

"How can you buy or sell the sky,
the warmth of the land?
...If we do not own the freshness of the air
and the sparkle of the water,
how can you buy them?
Every part of the earth is sacred to my
people.
Every shining pine needle, every sandy
shore, every mist in the dark woods,
every clearing, and every humming
insect is holy in the memory and
experience of my people...
This we know.
All things are connected.

Whatever befalls the earth befalls the sons of earth.
Man did not weave the web of life; he is merely a strand in it.
Whatever he does to the web, he does to himself."

CHIEF SEATTLE (1786-1866)

NATIVE AMERICAN

EARTH

I can hear its cry as it shifts and turns to alleviate pain. Its veins are injected with toxins, its skin breaks out in blisters in areas exposed to the elements lacking the protection of the trees. Caverns are gouged out filled with human waste; producing pain intense as searing knives penetrating its organs.

At night, it is kept awake by the cries of the various species whose habitats are destroyed. Acres of rainforests are under attack, resulting in a holocaust of barrenness. Fire storms are sweeping across the land, waves crashing on the shore. Those concerned about its safety now cry from the wilderness "Beware, beware!" Recognizing the urgency for our mother to be nourished back to health.

Poor Earth weeps at the sight of the children in slums walking on barren ground and those shut away in luxury condos chauffeured from the caverns of concrete parking stalls, their feet deprived of the intimacy of its soil.

KATHARINA NOLLA

Mother is digging up the vegetable patch, her skin looking flushed and absorbed, and I, remember the times when my head was young and the world still seemed a safe place and I, painted the blades of grass and the laughing sun looking down. I drew sketches of her sneakers, then still tied with laces, which she framed and hung in the hallway and said, "You will be the next Picasso, Jonathan." Mother is digging up the vegetable patch, her skin looking flushed and absorbed, and I, remember the times when my head was young and the world still seemed a safe place and I, painted the blades of grass and the laughing sun looking down. I drew sketches of her sneakers, then still tied with laces, which she framed and hung in the hallway and said, "You will be the next Picasso, Jonathan."

Her friend Ida laughs at Mother's bare hands "rooting" in the soil, wondering why she doesn't wear gloves.

"Because Earth likes to be caressed, exchanging its pleasure," she said.

I recall when we walked through the meadows and along the forest trails, looking for plantain and dandelion and other greens to be tossed into the salads, and we picked fiddleheads with their curled tips which I painted, but the finished result looked like little green snails instead of fiddles, because that's how I saw them.

Her favourite wild vegetable is stinging nettles, which she steams then chops up to be mixed into a sauce sautéed with garlic, or added to her bouillabaisse.

I have a secret stashed away. She doesn't know that I have unpacked my paints and canvasses from the basement. When she comes out of her nature trance and sees them spread out on the lawn, her eyes stare in surprise, and she exclaims, "Jonathan, you are painting," her eyes sparkling as she runs towards me.

I have been painting for several days, I tell her.

"Where are the paintings?"

"They are stashed in my room." She excitedly runs into the house to take a look. Upon closer inspection, she points and says, "This looks like Linda from the guesthouse."

"It is Linda."

But I don't tell her that Linda called to ask me out to a movie.

"I will come," I said and I am planning on taking her for cheesecake afterwards as I recall how she enjoys her sweets. Aren't you going to eat your desert, Jonathan, she would ask, and I would automatically slide the plate her way, with her fingers already eagerly poised with anticipated pleasure.

Leni

LIFE'S MESSAGE

"I am energy, the Venus rising, the great oracle. A deep cauldron that steams and bubbles. I infuse my energy into the tallest and the tiniest plant and composting particle. I cannot dispense the dosages that are compatible with you, but simply provide the energy. Your lesson is the art of balancing the ingredients.

A lesson researched in your own internal lab is a lesson that will not fail you. If you take too small a dose, your energy will fade. If you consume too much, this could create blockages that might choke you. An overdose could send you over the edge. Each time you draw excessively from the collective source, this will cause an imbalance in certain places for your fellow travellers. I myself, then suffer as I observe your gluttony that lacks generosity.

"If you want to be a giver, then give up some of your self-righteousness and be reminded that any suffering inflicted on others will eventually bounce back as an imbalance, until you get it right. This is how you can be of service.

"Once you complete your lessons, then oh my ... when you have learned to balance the ingredients and avoid harm to yourself and others, even Death will not frighten you then, but you will exit with gratitude, and this is the joy of my own reward. "Be kind to me and don't push me out of the way.

Be kind to each other and don't jostle each other out of the way, because you are in this together.

At times, you feel weary, standing in the shadow of obscurity, begging to have the answers to your lessons wrapped in a neat little package. But this cannot be done because the ultimate result then wouldn't be complete. For this you cannot pay any fee nor bribe the universe, nor each other.

"Ultimately, there is nothing standing in the way of completion. It all comes back to practice. When you plan to climb Mount Everest, the vision is the seed. Completing the vision requires practice to train your body into shape.

"Mine is not always an easy role when your chariot races out of control. At times there may seem too many obstacles standing in your way to fulfil your vision. But at the completion of your lesson you will arrive at the realization that the only obstacle has always been you. You will also realize that I am the force of your resurrection. You can draw a sword to challenge and battle with life but understand that life does not want to battle, it merely calls to be experienced. When you treat my relationship as a struggle, the messages will react accordingly.

"Life is designed to elevate you to your highest integrity and your ultimate passion and will always remain true to what it is."

PART IV

Jonathan

9 pm: Mother is planning a trip back to the West Coast, she asks if I care to come. I tell her I am going for a walk to Clover Point and have to think about this. The West Coast seems to have a way of sucking my energy, as if it couldn't get enough. Therefore, it might not be a good idea to expose myself to it for now.

Clover Point, Victoria

The stars are blinking their secrets. This is where Itak and I frequently used to meet and ponder on the mysteries of the heavens and ruminate on the scientific facts and equations, but in the end, conclude that without the mysteries there would be no incentive to stick around.

The mysteries are the challenges that extend to Itak's planet. They hide in the underbrush of the salal on Vargas Island, among the trees where I built my squatter's palace. They are imprinted in the church where father tried to figure out his own secrets with a vague look in his eyes, and where he told me never to give my power away.

But I did give my power away.

I surrendered it to my illness.

Memories surface. The Devil's words during our encounter, come to mind: "The problem arises when you become addicted to your play – to the point where you don't want to leave the stage but rather restrict yourself to your own repetitious script."

Back from the Point, I find mother still awake. I look at her and say, "I will come," but she seems preoccupied with her own thoughts.

Then she suddenly looks up and asks, "What did you just say?"

"I said I would come."

"I thought that's what I heard you say, but I wasn't sure."

Then she jumps up and bustles around, and I ask, "Isn't it time to go to bed?"

"I have to get things organized for the trip."

"If you bring forth what is within you,
What you bring forth will save you.
If you don't bring forth what
is within you,
What you don't bring forth will
destroy you."

GOSPEL OF ST. THOMAS

KATHARINA NOLLA

Leni

West Coast: Vancouver Island

PEG'S cottages that had weathered years of winter storms
and the pounding waves spraying the windows are now a
mere memory of the past, her acres of property declared
a provincial park. But Jonathan and I found the old trail
through the forest and paid homage in honour to her
memory.

After a long stretch of life's twists and turns, I feel
we have arrived.

Arrived, where?

The answer is: At the end of the search, where it all
began.

10 a.m.

Between trendy B&Bs, I discovered a rustic cottage reminiscent of Peg's. Dewdrops settled on the spider webs
outside the window, look like precious pearls illuminated
by the morning sun. Jonathan is still soundlessly asleep in
the room next to mine, which evokes a sense of peace as
during his childhood days that were young and pure. The
journey has a beginning and an end, and then a beginning
again. And this time around, we can leave a lot of baggage
behind.

The waves are rolling in, spreading out in unison like a giant cape across the beach. Then fold up in participating back to fit into the chorus of the ocean.

The sun is smiling in the sky. As I stretch out on the beach shielding my face with my straw hat, the rays filtering through the hat's perforations create illusory miniature cathedral windows and display designs of jewels for me to enjoy.

Now later in the day, Jonathan and I are standing on Radar Hill. A wind is sweeping over its crest, ruffling my skirt and sliding its invisible fingers through our hair while Jonathan and I are waiting for the sun to set.

"If the ancient Greeks had been here, they would have chosen to build their temple on this site," I say. The sun explodes into a fiery disk. Then we watch it descend, round and gigantic, wading on the horizon of the ocean, before it gradually sinks inch by inch into the powder-blue misty sea, leaving an orange streak in the sky.

I reflect back on the vision of pushing the cabooses up the hill and the priestess' words reminding me to open the windows. She confirmed that the world out there is quite delightful, and I feel that the pushing is now over. I remind myself that this human mind is a cornucopia of abundance and it mirrors wonders not seen before. I begin to hum.

Jonathan's voice breaks through my reverie. "Brahms's lullaby," he says. "I remember you singing it to me."

We walk down the hill.

The beginning.

"Tomorrow Linda is going to arrive on the bus," Jonathan says.

"Oh my, then let's go and pick up a cheesecake in the morning!"

There is a trunk at home in my basement
The trunk has a lock
The lock has a key.
The trunk is now wide open.

Then there's just us – Jonathan and me, silently walking along the beach accompanied by the wind and the sound of the waves.

Washed-up logs point ghostly fingers into the approaching night, while silhouettes of distant islands slumber in their dream state and the heavens curve an intimate dome, embracing the world below.

When we walk into the cottage, the flames are dancing in the fireplace the cats preoccupied in their task of grooming their fur.

"Just in time for dinner," our hostess Min calls out.
It smells delicious.

The End